Anna, Analyst

Yellow Dog (an imprint of Great Plains Publications)
1173 Wolseley Avenue
Winnipeg, MB R3G 1H1
www.greatplains.mb.ca

Great Plains Publications gratefully acknowledges the financial support
provided for its publishing program by the Government of Canada through
the Canada Book Fund; the Canada Council for the Arts; the Province of
Manitoba through the Book Publishing Tax Credit and the Book Publisher
Marketing Assistance Program; and the Manitoba Arts Council.

Design & Typography by Relish New Brand Experience
Printed in Canada by Friesens

Library and Archives Canada Cataloguing in Publication

Title: Anna, analyst : a novel / Patti Edgar
Names: Edgar, Patti, author.
Identifiers: Canadiana (print) 20210101385 | Canadiana (ebook) 20210101393 |
     ISBN 9781773370569 (softcover) | ISBN 9781773370576 (ebook)
Classification: LCC PS8609.D54 A56 2021 | DDC jC813/.6‚Äîdc23

ENVIRONMENTAL BENEFITS STATEMENT

Great Plains Publications saved the following
resources by printing the pages of this book on
chlorine free paper made with 100% post-consumer
waste.

TREES	WATER	ENERGY	SOLID WASTE	GREENHOUSE GASES
4	330	2	15	1,780
FULLY GROWN	GALLONS	MILLION BTUs	POUNDS	POUNDS

Environmental impact estimates were made using the Environmental Paper Network
Paper Calculator 4.0. For more information visit www.papercalculator.org.

Canadä

FSC
www.fsc.org

MIX

Paper from
responsible sources

FSC® C016245

Anna, Analyst

Patti Edgar

yellow dog

For my family

CHAPTER ONE

A History of Graphology

On my last day of elementary school, I unfolded the note I'd written on my first: "A tortoise always sticks its neck out." The penciled letters had smudged together a little. But that didn't matter. A six-year-old with sloppy printing and no respect for blue lines had already messed it up. I remembered how Mom had forced me to copy her words out during breakfast on my first day at Hidden Heights Elementary. And she must have slipped the piece of paper into the front pocket of my backpack on that last morning of fifth grade. I found it while searching for the key I needed to lock my bike to the rack in the schoolyard.

Little kids darted everywhere, hanging upside down on the monkey bars, shrieking and laughing. The June sun warmed my bare arms and the air smelled like fresh-cut dandelions. I turned the key in the lock, then shoved it into my backpack along with the old note. Like my tortoises, Nachos and Salsa, I preferred the comforts of a familiar shell.

"Can you believe we'll be going to middle school, Anna?"

Lana hovered over me in a satiny black dress, her usually straight hair twisted onto the top of her head like a cinnamon bagel. I stood up, lugging my backpack over my shoulder. Lana stared at me, blinking rapidly, like maybe a fruit fly was lodged under one of her lids.

"What's wrong with your eyes?" I asked.

"It makes a big difference, doesn't it? It's called Black Iris."

"Is that like pink eye?"

"No. Gross." She blinked again, slowly, keeping her eyes closed for a moment and I noticed her thick, dark lashes. And then I realized it. She was wearing mascara. Mascara! In two months we'd be in a new school and Lana was already doing something without me.

"Isn't mascara itchy?" I said, rubbing one of my eyes to mess with her. "I hate it when my eyes are itchy. I just want to scratch them right out. So, so itchy."

Lana scrunched up her nose. "Stop that, Anna. I don't want my mascara to be all smeared for the graduation ceremony. Where's your dress?"

I took off my bike helmet and tried to unknot my curls with my fingertips. That mascara bothered me, but I was sure we would always be the Banana Twins. (Because Anna and Lana rhyme with banana. That was more of a first-day-of-elementary-school thing. We didn't call ourselves that on the last day.)

I looked down at my red plaid leggings and faded grey T-shirt that I'd picked up off the floor that morning. "They make us wear those big black gowns anyway. Who cares what's underneath?"

Lana sighed. "You'll always be the same old Anna."

Lana and I walked to the fifth-grade doors. Some of the girls waiting in the shade of the building squealed when they noticed Lana's mascara, sucking her into their circle of shiny dresses. Even the boys standing by the soccer goalposts wore pants without holes in the knees. A few kicked a ball around.

But then there was Evan in shorts and a faded T-shirt with a picture of mustachioed astronaut Chris Hadfield on it. I tried not to stare at the red scars on Evan's leg from his bike accident. He leaned against the ledge of the cement retaining wall and sort of looked up at the clouds. Evan never played soccer. He was planning to go to space one day. That dream marked him early on as weird, especially since he used to do strange things when we were little, like practice holding his breath in buckets of water and responding to teachers in an alien-like language. Now he just played video games in his basement.

"What are you doing this summer?" Evan asked. He tucked a flop of dark hair off his forehead and behind his left ear so he could see me better.

"Hole-in-ones at Putter's Paradise, of course. Lana and I are going to bike there, probably every day." I glanced over at Lana, who was laughing with Harlow Godfrey, the tallest girl in school. Harlow's biggest claim to fame was her palatal expander.

"That dumpy minigolf place?" Evan said. "It was fine when we were little, but the course is way too easy now." He scratched at the scar on his leg. I instantly felt bad about bringing up biking. Evan had been riding his bike when a car turning right hit him. Actually, the car slammed into a bike trailer, which was attached to Evan's bike, but luckily the only thing he was hauling were model rockets. His mom had driven Evan to school every day since.

"If you bring Nachos and Salsa to the park you should drop by house," said Evan. "My mom is growing too many veggies in the backyard. The tortoises could eat as much lettuce as they want."

"Okay, but Lana will be with me," I warned.

Evan wasn't much of a Lana fan. We used to all play together when we were little because we live close to each other, but earlier this year he called her vapid, which was a word I needed to look up and it wasn't very flattering.

"Fine, bring Lana," he said. "She can eat as much lettuce as she wants too."

Once we got into our classroom, I noticed Ms. Kozak had scribbled 'Congratulations!' on the whiteboard in fat loopy letters. That morning, we had to prepare the classroom for the next group of fifth graders, which sounded like a job for the custodial staff, but we were technically held captive inside until the graduation ceremony, and our teacher ran out of things to teach us about a month ago.

Ms. Kozak told me and Lana to clean out the junk inside the giant, musty-smelling cupboards on the back wall. Lana complained about the dust as she eyed Harlow Godfrey and the other girls in satiny dresses taking down posters and artwork. Evan organized the science equipment on the table by the windows, clanging together beakers and vials.

"I watched *Ponyo* last night," said Lana as she pulled out a cardboard box full of DVDs with titles like *Hygiene for Healthy Kids*. "Now I've seen every one of Hayao Miyazaki's movies. You should give Japanese anime another chance."

I dropped an ancient textbook onto the floor with a thump. Japanese anime was Lana's newest obsession. "No way. They're too weird." Everything about those cartoon films bugged me, especially the way the characters' mouths moved in a way that didn't really match the words.

"Harlow says she likes *Spirited Away*," said Lana. "We're planning a Miyazaki marathon this summer."

"If you run a marathon against Harlow Godfrey, she's going to beat you," I said. "She's got legs like a giraffe."

Lana glanced nervously at Harlow and her friends. "Shush. She'll hear you."

"So?"

Lana pulled an old-fashioned pencil sharpener out of the cupboard that had a crank handle on it. She tried to turn it, but it jammed. "Why does Ms. Kozak keep so much junk in these cupboards? It's like no one has gone in here in a hundred years. My dress is going to be all dusty and I'm nervous enough about the graduation ceremony."

I tossed a broken yellow ruler into the trash can.

"You love being the centre of attention. Remember the piano recital? The tap dance show? You always do great on stage. I'm the one who's going to fall off that stupid pony."

Lana smiled, either remembering her performances or the time the graduation pony bucked off nervous Laura Nelson. "You always know what to say, Anna." She held up the pencil sharpener. "Do you think I should bring this thing home?" Lana had a talent for fixing stuff with gears. She used to take apart her toys and even repaired my broken music box once.

"You could easily fix that old thing," I said.

Lana set it aside for later and started to sort through the ancient DVDs.

To get to the rest of the textbooks, I needed to reach the top shelf. I climbed onto a chair and coughed a few times as I reached further and further back into the cupboard, bringing out math and science books with beat-up covers and torn pages. I felt a book that was different. It was leathery, kind of like my tortoises. I pulled it out and wiped dust off with my sleeve. The cover was plain and dark burgundy. *The Guide to Graphology* was printed on the spine in gold letters. I flipped it open and read a random page.

"Look at this book, Lana." I jumped down off the chair. "It says you can learn lots about someone from studying their handwriting. Write something so I can see if it works."

"No way. I'm not going to be your science experiment." Lana pulled the mascara out of her pocket and held it up to me. "You can try this on in the bathroom if you want. It would really change the look of your face."

I snorted. "I'm not going to be *your* science experiment. Besides, I don't understand why everybody thinks they need to change. It's only middle school. What's the big difference between fifth grade and sixth grade anyway?"

"Only about a million differences, Anna."

I kept flipping through the book, glancing at sketches showing different ways of shaping letters. I whipped back to the first page, which promised me insight into the "abilities and abnormalities of mankind." I glanced up at the whiteboard and compared Ms. Kozak's handwriting to a page showing handwritten letters inside the book. The wide loop of her C indicated wastefulness.

"Ms. Kozak, can I keep one of these old books?" I asked. She pushed a pile of our old test papers off her desk and into the recycling bin.

"Take as many as you want," she said. "They're headed for the dump."

CHAPTER TWO

Changing Elements in Handwriting

W e heard the principal's shrill voice over the speakers as we lined up behind the curtains on stage, drowning in black gowns and graduation hats.

It was dark. There was lots of whispering and giggling. A few kids with dander allergies were pre-emptively sneezing because of the nearby pony. Lana was in front of me. Behind me, a girl called Maddison was wiping her nose on the sleeve of her gown, leaving a shimmering slug-like trail.

I was thinking about Lana's offer to share her mascara, that maybe it meant things between us would be all right in middle school, even if we didn't agree on the usefulness of Japanese cartoon movies or Harlow Godfrey.

Anna and Lana. Best friends. Inseparable.

Then Lana turned and whispered to me: "These are our very last moments of elementary school. Can you believe it? Everything is going to be *so* different next year."

"Middle school is not going to change me," I whispered.

Lana shrugged. "Change can be good. Besides, we've got two whole months of summer to enjoy first. No day camps."

Lana had talked her mom into letting her skip weeks of day camps this summer because she'd supposedly outgrown it, while my mom said she'd be watching me at home instead since she was freshly unemployed.

"We should go to Putter's Paradise on our own this summer," I said, hoping to remind her of the highlight of previous day camps. "We should also bring Nachos and Salsa to the park by my house a lot. They need fresh air and exercise. You can carry Nachos. Or Salsa. Whichever one you want. I can't carry both."

"Anna, they're turtles. They don't need fresh air and exercise."

"They're not turtles, they're tortoises," I hissed at Lana, a little louder than I meant to. "And you clearly don't know much about chelonians."

Lana shook her head. "Key- what?"

Evan, who was in front of Lana in the line, corrected her. "It's key-loan-ian. Now be quiet. We're almost up." I think Lana blushed, but it was hard to tell in the dark.

The line started to move and we shuffled forward. Fifth graders go on the stage in pairs, with one as the pony rider and the other leading the pony by its reins. The teacher picked our partners, so Lana was with Evan and I was stuck with Maddison.

Lana whispered: "This lady my mom knows from work needs a dog sitter this summer. She's going on a road trip and they can't take the dog because he gets carsick. My mom told me about it this morning. I'm so excited. She says I might get the job, especially since she's working from home this summer."

A dog? That took me by surprise. "You can't look after a dog this summer. We'd never see each other. Dogs aren't allowed on the greens at Putter's Paradise, and a dog could really hurt Nachos and Salsa, so you couldn't come to my house. My dad is always warning me about dogs when I take them to the park."

Lana brushed a hair off the sleeve of her black gown. "But this lady is going to pay me and I hardly have to do anything. I could save up for a whole new look for middle school."

"What's wrong with your 'look' now?"

"It's middle school, Anna. I realize you don't know anything about fashion, but I've been getting tips from Harlow. She showed me all these sites on her phone. And Mom says if I save up enough money, I can have my own phone too."

A phone? That made me jealous. I wanted to put daily snaps of Nachos and Salsa online and my mom wouldn't even let me do that with *her* phone. Everyone puts pictures of clothes and makeup online. Tortoises with attitude? That's original.

"But you don't actually have to be with this dog all the time, right?" I asked. "We can still go to Putter's Paradise. Won't your mom watch him sometimes?"

Lana shushed me because we were getting close to the front of the line.

I started to get hot under that satiny gown and could feel dampness around the neckline. What about taking Nachos and Salsa to the park? What about improving our minigolf skills?

I glanced around me to see if there was anyone else who might be a good tortoise transporter. This wasn't exactly a reptile-friendly graduating class. Evan and Lana slipped between the curtain and onto the stage. It was almost my turn. I turned around and stared at Maddison, wondering if she could handle a tortoise like Nachos.

She brushed her blonde, chin-length hair out of her worried, watery eyes. "I'm probably allergic to ponies," she said. "I've never been around one before. I'm allergic to cats and dogs. Tree nuts too."

I could hear the principal announcing Evan and Lana's names. "Are you allergic to tortoises?" I asked.

"Do they have dander?" Maddison gave me a nudge. "Go, Anna. It's our turn. Remember you're the one riding."

I pushed my way through the musty curtain and walked on stage, where the assistant principal helped me climb the stepstool and mount the grey pony. Yes, a pony. My principal was over-the-top about everything. There were probably pages and pages in the handwriting book about people like her and their massive, loopy, over-the-top handwriting.

Maddison took hold of the reins and pulled me across the stage, sneezing and rubbing her nose on her gown. I looked out into the dimly lit audience to see my dad waving his arms at me and the repeated flashes of my mom's special-occasions-only camera.

The principal, standing at a podium, announced our names. She narrowed her eyes at Maddison, who was splattering her mucous across the stage, but pasted on a fake smile when we were close enough to reach for our diplomas. And then someone above us released confetti, which fluttered down and stuck to the snot on Maddison's sleeve.

I should have felt excited at that point, like sitting on that pony with confetti in my hair and everyone clapping meant the start of something exciting and grown up. But I only felt a kind of sadness that the gym, the school, these teachers, all these kids, and maybe even Lana didn't need me anymore. That I was about as important to them as the old book on handwriting analysis that Ms. Kozak was going to throw in the trash.

One of the teachers helped me off the pony and pointed out our folding seats among the graduating class.

"Sorry about all that," whispered Maddison. "I left my antihistamines on the bus."

"Don't worry about it," I said. I was secretly relieved Maddison, since she lived at least a bus ride away from our neighborhood, was not eligible to be a tortoise transporter.

CHAPTER THREE

The Basic Tendencies

I didn't open my curtains on the first morning of summer. Instead, I lay on my back next to the tortoise habitat, holding up *The Guide to Graphology* as close to the glow of the basking lamp as I could. The reptile posters on my walls looked all shadowy. The blue carpet felt soft between my bare toes. Salsa was nibbling on a chunk of cucumber and Nachos was hiding in her cardboard box. I could almost pretend summer and all the changes coming weren't out there, despite the sliver of sunlight pushing through the slit in the curtains.

Nachos and Salsa's habitat took up a lot of space. It was kind of shaped like a small bathtub, but it was black and filled with dirt and driftwood and a few plants. Nachos and Salsa were Hermann's tortoises, so relatively small. I think that's why Lana always called them turtles. But tortoises don't swim and they don't need much more than a bowl of water. Nachos was the one with the pattern on her shell that reminded me of a bowl of tortilla chips, and Salsa was the other one, because salsa goes really well with nachos. I got my tortoises from my dad, who says a university roommate left them behind to go backpacking through India. I renamed them because their original old lady names didn't fit them.

I was on the first chapter of the book. It was called "General Introduction to Graphology." The author used a lot of old-fashioned words that I didn't know, like "capricious" and "aesthetic." And I didn't have Mom's phone handy to look those up. There were some tips on how to understand people just from looking at their handwriting. Like this one: "Handwriting that replicates the samples in a workbook or instructor's blackboard indicates a deficiency in personality and imagination, while penmanship with irregular tendencies reflects shifting moods and a lack of attention to detail." I tried to remember Lana's handwriting. Likely she is closer to the boring end of the scale.

Dad knocked and then pushed open the door. He plugged his nose, waving his hand in front of his face dramatically. My dad has glasses and almost no hair. He hardly ever stands up straight because he's so tall that he has to bend down to talk to everyone. He kind of looks like a cartoon turtle, which is one thing I really like about him.

"Holy tortoise poop," Dad said. "We're going to have to do something about that."

"It's not that bad," I said. Tortoises don't have much of an odour, except their droppings, which kind of have a damp, pine forest scent, unless you leave them too long. But it had been a while since anyone had cleaned the habitat out. The water bowl looked a little fuzzy.

Dad crouched down and Salsa waddled over to say hello. Dad gave her a pat and took a closer peek through the opening in the cardboard box to see Nachos.

"What's the book about?" Dad asked.

"Graphology."

"Is that a math thing?" He winked.

But before I could explain to him that graphology is not math at all, Dad started lecturing. "This is a mess. Problems happen when we don't take care of the habitat. I'm going to refill the water bowl. Let's open the curtains and give them some natural light."

I reached over and gave Salsa a little scratch on her shell. "I've been really busy with the end of school."

"Maybe we should move them back into the living room," Dad said as he shoved open the curtains, practically blinding me. "This seems to be too much responsibility for you."

"It's not. I'll clean the habitat."

"I still haven't booked the annual checkup with the vet," Dad mumbled.

"The one with the snakes?"

Dad kind of stepped back and hunched into himself even more. If he were a tortoise, he would have stuck his head in his shell. I could tell he was also thinking about Dr. O'Sullivan's snake collection. We both like reptiles, but we don't like snakes. I'm not sure why the slithery things are even considered reptiles. But Dr. O'Sullivan understood tortoises and her office was close to our house.

"I'll make the appointment," I said. I knew the number was on Mom's phone.

"Are you sure? You won't forget?"

"I promise."

When Dad left to refill the bowl, I finished the first chapter of the book. I'd get to my promises later. There was a whole part about how even though people might change their handwriting a little because of their mood or because they are in a rush, the pen strokes are basically still the same. You'd have to do a real overhaul on a person to have new handwriting. Like, if you hypnotize someone and make them pretend to be someone else, maybe a queen or a pirate, their handwriting will temporarily change. But when you snapped your fingers, they'd be back to being themselves—handwriting and all.

That made me think about Lana and her mascara. Had she changed permanently, or was Harlow Godfrey a kind of temporary hypnotist? I felt like calling Lana, but then I remembered her mom had promised to take her to the mall to check out new phones. If Lana got that dog sitting job, she'd be too busy to go with me to Putter's Paradise this summer. And Lana's really good at minigolf. Once she bounced a ball off a gnome on the eighth hole and the ball leaped across the fake creek and plopped right into the sixteenth hole. But at the graduation ceremony Lana seemed to care more about a strange dog and Harlow Godfrey's fashion advice than spending time minigolfing with her best friend.

I glanced back down at *The Guide to Graphology* and thought about Lana's too-neat handwriting. I wondered if the way she wrote her letters would give me any clues. There was nothing with her handwriting on it at my house, and she'd already said there was no way she'd let me experiment on her. But I thought of a sneaky way to get a sample.

CHAPTER FOUR

Acquiring a Specimen

The next day spit summer rain, so Lana arrived at my front door with a huge, hot pink umbrella. The big gobs of black mascara on her lashes hadn't even gotten all wet and runny.

Once we reached my room, Lana scrunched up her nose and shot a sideway glance at the habitat. She flopped down on my bed without even saying hello to Nachos and Salsa. "Did I tell you I fixed that pencil sharpener? The gears were just jammed."

"You're great at repairing stuff," I said. I squatted over the habitat, offering a wilted piece of kale to Salsa, who didn't seem interested. Looking at the scuzzy water made me realize that I had forgotten to clean up and to make the vet appointment. I'd do it once Lana went home. "But those things are obsolete. We have automatic pencil sharpeners now. There's even digital pencils."

Lana shrugged, like maybe she agreed with me.

I tried to coax Nachos out of her shoebox with the kale, but she ignored me. "When does the dog sitting job start? How much are they paying you?" I asked. Lana does not like talking to most adults. She's okay with teachers but quiet around my mom and dad. I guessed she wouldn't know any details about the job.

"I'll figure out when I meet the dog."

I scooched closer to Lana. "That's a big mistake. What if they think you'll watch their dog for, like, a dollar a day?"

"My mom is going to arrange everything for me. I'm sure they pay more than a dollar."

"Will it be enough to get you a whole new look and a phone?"

"I'm not worried about it."

I threw my hands up in the air for dramatic effect, like I couldn't believe how trusting she was being. "Will your mom promise you'll go on walks three times a day? Or toss a stick? Because I heard dogs really like to play fetch. You should make sure that's not expected of you."

Even when we were little, Lana did not enjoy playing fetch at the park. Especially not with Nachos and Salsa, who didn't seem as interested in retrieving sticks as I had hoped.

"I'm not walking a dog three times a day. That's too much work." Lana rearranged my pillows and I could tell she was concerned.

"You can't count on your mom to look out for your best interests. She's probably happy to have you busy all summer, especially since you convinced her you're too old for day camp."

Now Lana leaned against my headboard, pressing a pillow to her stomach. "I hate talking to adults. It makes me feel sick. How do I figure that stuff out without talking to them?"

"You should have a contract, get it all down in writing. Then you don't need to go through your mom."

"You write it, Anna. You're better at writing stuff than me. I don't even remember the dog's name."

But I wanted *her* to do this. I needed *her* handwriting. I had to think fast. "I can help you, but we'll need two copies. One for you and one for the lady. That's the way these things are done. We'll both do it at the same time and I'll keep one here and you bring the other one to her."

That afternoon we wrote up a contract, and although the handwriting on the copy I kept was genuinely Lana's, there were quite a lot of my personal touches in the wording. She took my copy home and promised to fill in the dog's name, once she figured it out.

> Myself, Lana Livingstone, enters into a contract, on this June 28, to take care of the dog _____ for six weeks. No more than one walk a day required, with three breaks for me, including one hour for lunch and two 20-minute breaks for personal time. During my personal time, the dog will watch television from inside his crate, but nothing involving characters with annoying voices. I will be paid at a rate of $50 a day and all snacks and meals for the dog will be pre-made and labelled. I will not be required to play fetch, visit bodies of water, nor administer an EpiPen in case of serious allergies. Time spent outside will be limited to no more than one half hour, on leash, and flea control will be pre-applied. The dog can NOT, under any circumstances, play with a zax. Any failure to abide by the provisions will result in termination of the contract.

The sample was perfect. She'd filled a whole page of lined paper. I tricked her into putting a zax in there, which I told her is an annoyingly squeaky chew toy but is actually a roofing tool I learned about from playing Scrabble. That way I made sure she'd written every letter in the alphabet. I was hoping that, as a bonus, the dog lady would be offended by the contract, cancel the pooch-sitting job, and Lana would never be able to buy a phone and a change of look before middle school. We could spend every day at Putter's Paradise, knocking balls around the peeling fake grass.

CHAPTER FIVE

Working Out an Analysis

My dad quit drinking coffee this past spring. So each day my mom, who was never much of a morning person to begin with and got even crabbier when she lost her office job, bumped around the kitchen like a blind lizard with a thorn in its foot. Dad used to make the coffee. Now he was making fancy breakfasts in his bathrobe. I liked being on the receiving end of the crepes and homemade granola, but my mom said she hated it because she was forced to brew her own coffee and was left with a bunch of extra dishes after he left for work.

That morning, Dad was whistling and flipping pancakes. Mom elbowed him out of the way to reach for the coffee filters and scowled as she measured out the scoops of grinds. Her dark hair was a mess of curls pinned up on the top of her head.

"You should really quit caffeine," Dad told her. "Takes years off."

She growled back at him. "Once I get a new job, I'm going to get a coffee maker with a timer. Then it will be like the old days. I'll wake up to a fresh pot."

Dad gave her a kiss on the top of her head and put a stack of pancakes in the oven to warm. The heat from the oven steamed up his glasses. "Did you remember to clean the tortoise habitat, Anna?"

"I'll do it right after breakfast," I said. "Is it okay if I bike to Putter's Paradise some day this week with Lana?"

I know there are fancier minigolf courses in the world, with pink castles and flowing moats and whirring windmills. But the thing I like about this one is it's not fancy at all. The green carpet is peeling up in many corners and the big, weathered windmill doesn't turn unless you spin it yourself. The fake waterfall is usually broken, so the water pools in the creek and has red scum on the top. In the patches of grass around the course, there are even little green, dome-shaped sprinklers, which look like tortoises if you squint.

"It's much too far to go on your own, Anna," Mom said. "I was nervous enough about letting you bike the five blocks to school this spring."

"Yeah, I know. Half the time you were following me in the minivan."

Lana's mom let her do practically anything. Lana even wore a crop top on the first day of the third grade. My parents had always kept their spotlight shining hot on me, but ever since Mom got laid off, it had gotten worse. It was like I was under one of my tortoises' basking lamps.

"But you're going to let me bike alone to middle school, right? I can't have my mom stalking me."

Mom frowned into her empty coffee mug. "I'm not sure that's a safe choice. It's too far away. I'll drive you to the new school, okay?"

"It's not that far," I said, wishing I hadn't asked while she was waiting for the coffee pot to fill up. "Besides, a tortoise needs to stick its neck out, right? You made me write that down once."

"That idiom was about taking *emotional* chances," Mom said. "Not physical ones."

"I thought it was about tortoises," I mumbled.

Mom didn't start to come around until she was on her second cup and Dad and I were eating pancakes at the kitchen island. She sat down on a stool and exchanged a 'look' with Dad that made it hard to swallow my syrupy chunk of pancake. That look was always followed by a serious discussion.

"We had something we wanted to talk to you about," Mom said.

Dad continued: "We wanted to discuss the additional duties that a family takes on when a pet comes into their lives—"

Suddenly I knew what he meant. "Cheese!" I shouted. Mom and Dad looked confused. "We can call my new tortoise Cheese. Of course, I would have to make sure the name fits. Wait. Where would I find a rescue tortoise?"

Mom snorted as she sipped her coffee.

"We are thinking it might be time for a different kind of change," Dad said. "Those tortoises ended up in our lives by accident. My old college roommate has been in touch. He's no longer a free-spirited, globe-trotting backpacker. He's settled down and is ready to take the tortoises back."

I stared at Dad in shock. "What? I'm not giving up Nachos and Salsa."

"It's a lot of work for a child," said Mom.

"I'm not a little kid anymore. I'm going to middle school."

"Exactly," Mom said. "In a few years you'll be a teenager and will feel differently about how you want to spend your time. We only want what's best for the tortoises."

I turned to Dad. "Seriously, you are agreeing with her?" He had these tortoises first, for years after his roommate left them behind. He couldn't possibly want to give them back. I knew I could get him on my side. "The guy *abandoned* them."

"Frank seems to genuinely want to give them a good, permanent home," Dad said. "He's got a farm, I think. Just out of town."

"We can talk about this again later," Mom said. "You don't need to focus your life on these tortoises right now and you're going to outgrow them eventually."

"I will never feel differently about Nachos and Salsa," I said. "They're my family."

Dad adjusted his glasses. "Let's concentrate on proper care, for now. Have you booked their checkup yet?"

That made me feel guilty. I hadn't even remembered to clean the habitat that morning. And I'd forgotten all about my promise to call the vet.

Mom tried one more time to get me on her side. "Tortoises don't feel affection for their caretakers. They aren't like, I don't know… not the same kind of pet as a dog. They live a long time and need a clean, permanent home where they can be safe and have proper vet care. We can't pass up this opportunity."

I pushed my chair away from the table. "Nachos and

Salsa care about me. And you're right, they aren't anything like a dumb dog!"

Alone in my room, I offered Nachos a Swiss chard leaf and then scratched Salsa while she sunned herself under the basking lamp. I needed to call Lana to tell her about what happened at breakfast. I dug a Post-It note out of my desk drawer, wrote a little reminder to myself to scrub out the habitat, and stuck it on Salsa's shell. Then I slipped out to get my mom's phone off her bedside table and snuck back to my room.

I told Lana all about my mother's betrayal. Lana seemed to miss the point. "I agree with your mom. A dog is probably a lot more fun than a couple of slow-moving turtles."

"Nachos and Salsa are not slow. They're deliberate." I walked over to my bedside drawer and pulled out the dog sitting contract we had written up.

"I don't even know what you mean," said Lana.

"It means they have a plan. What did the dog lady say when you gave her the contract we wrote?"

Lana hesitated before answering. "I showed my mom first. She asked me what a zax was and I couldn't even remember. Then she offered to call the lady instead. She sorted out all the details for me. Isn't that great?"

Lana hadn't stuck to our plan! I felt myself get mad at her all over again. "And you always say *my* mom is the one who thinks she needs to help with everything."

"Well, it's all worked out now," Lana said. "This dog sitting job is going to be so good. I'm going to have a couple hundred dollars by the end of July and more in August. Do you think I should get the same phone as Harlow? She says there's a cool app for chatting and sending photos."

"I don't care which phone you get, Lana."

After we'd hung up, I thought about how confusing it was that Lana was suddenly caring all about mascara and money. She was never like that before. We used to spend hours in the summer hanging out in day camps, or at the park or the pool, not even thinking about that stuff. I looked at the contract, wishing the dog lady could have at least seen it, because if she had, she would never have let Lana dog sit. I dug my graphology book out from under my bed and decided to take a closer look at Lana's handwriting.

I flipped through chapter two of *The Guide to Graphology*, pausing to read about all the prisoners, job applicants, and nutty people who'd been test subjects for the author. Then I jumped ahead to the third chapter, which had a section on the first and last letters of a word. It seemed as good a place as any to start, and there were helpful pictures showing examples of different styles of letters with a note on each one's meaning. Because the first and last letters are not squished between other letters in a word, it makes sense that they can be unique to the writer. And the first letter in a name is practically a fingerprint, identifying you to the world. I studied Lana Livingstone's signature at the bottom of the contract for a while, and then the word "Myself" at the top of the page, hunting through the pages in the book for matches. I had to pay a lot of attention to how each letter fit between the blue lines on the paper. Eventually I wrote my analysis:

The test subject began her writing sample with the letter M. The first stroke of this letter dropped way below the blue line and to the left, showing that she is ambitious and manipulative. Wide, fat lettering indicates a writer who likes to speak about herself a lot and doesn't care about whether anyone else is listening. The first letter in her signature is L. The letter is all bent over to the right, showing that she is overly sensitive about things. She ends her name with a lower case "a." It's got a kind of hook on the end that loops around and points back to the name, showing a sense of self-importance. This concludes the initial analysis of Test Subject Number One (aka Lana Livingstone).

I reread it a few times. I glanced over at Salsa with the sticky note on her shell and felt doubtful, and a little sad. Maybe handwriting analysis isn't something you should do when your parents are selfishly blind to your desire for a third tortoise and your best friend is pushing a smelly, panting dog on you instead. And maybe you should read the whole book, including the really dull parts, and not just skip to chapter three. Because Lana was coming across as pretty self-centered, not exactly the person I thought of as my best friend. I stuffed the analysis and the book into my bedside drawer, hoping to forget the little ball of guilt forming in my chest.

CHAPTER SIX

Signs, Symbols, and Gestures

That first week of summer, Mom asked me if I wanted to go through her old cookbooks and learn how to whip something up from scratch. She had piled a stack of tattered cookbooks on the kitchen island and was flipping through one called *Vegetarian Casseroles*.

"Unless you have a cookbook dedicated to creating unique cuisine for the picky tortoise, I'm not interested," I said.

"What about knitting? I could teach you how to make this cute tea cozy." Mom reached for a yellowing folder and dug out a page torn from a magazine. In the picture, a hand reached out to plop a "cozy" made of multi-coloured yarn over a helpless teapot.

"No tortoise needs a sweater that ugly," I said.

Mom looked disappointed, but she didn't mention giving away Nachos and Salsa, so I relaxed a little.

On Saturday, the phone rang. Mom squished up her face at the smell when she came through the door of my room. I felt a tug of guilt as she passed me the phone. It was Lana. Ambitious, self-absorbed Lana told me her mom wanted to take us to the mall to try on new clothes. I explained that she had to help me take the tortoises to the park first, which was the only place my parents allowed me to bring them. I wasn't going to let Lana manipulate *me*. Lana complained a bit about this, but finally agreed, so I decided that handwriting analysis had its uses.

Lana and I walked to the little park about a block downhill from my house, each carefully holding a tortoise. I could feel my mom staring at me all the way down the street. She's okay with that little park because there's a nosey old lady who lives across from it. Mrs. DeJong does crosswords by the window all day and will call up my mom if anything suspicious is happening, such as neighbours mowing their front lawns in a diagonal pattern or teenagers kissing on the park bench. I think my mom is going to be just like her one day. She already plays Sudoku on her phone.

Lana was holding Salsa with both hands and going on and on about a store Harlow Godfrey told her to check out with cute tops, cute skirts, and cute socks. I glanced down at my cut-offs and the tie-dye t-shirt we'd made together last summer. All the colours had mixed together to form an unpleasant brownish grey. Not cute. Nothing about me was ever cute. I noticed that Lana was still wearing mascara, but I was trying my best not to bug her about it because I felt like I was more mature than I was at the start of the summer. And she was carrying around Salsa, just like she did last year.

"What's so important about having cute clothes for middle school?" I asked.

"I want to make a good impression. There's going to be kids from three different schools going there. It won't be the same old faces, you know what I mean? And we get lockers."

I noticed the lockers when we did the tour last month. Right away, I got nervous about having to memorize the combination for the lock. I also noticed all the anti-bullying posters. They were everywhere. Why would they need those unless there were bullies? Not that I would put up with anything like that from anyone, but weirdos like Evan and Maddison, they aren't as tough inside as me. I got all worried for them.

"I liked elementary school," I said. "We didn't need to lock things up because there were no bullies to swipe your stuff. And there wasn't even much homework. There's probably going to be mountains of it in middle school." Lana shrugged so I kept talking. "When are you going to get this dog? Are you going to have to play fetch with it?"

"Next week. I decided that throwing a ball for a dog will probably be a lot more fun than throwing a ball for a lazy turtle that will never ever bring it back to you. After all, I'm getting paid to hang around all summer and not do much."

I ignored Lana's comment because when I insisted the tortoises could play fetch, I was pretty little. It seemed unfair to bring it up now. "I guess everything is different when you're making money," I said. I secretly wished someone was paying me to do something.

"Have you met this dog?" I asked.

"Nope. I hope it's a cute little one. Like those short-haired ones with big ears that you can carry around in a purse. I think they are called chihuahuas. I've always wanted one of those."

"Yuck, no. Those are just rats you can dress up."

"Yeah, because turtles are *so* adorable," Lana said, but I could tell she wasn't really on my side by the tone of her voice.

When we reached the little park, Evan was there. Not surprising, because he lives across the street. When we were little, we all used to run between the clusters of lilac bushes pretending we'd survived a zombie takeover. Now Evan was crouched down over something in the grass. When he stepped back, I realized it was a model rocket, and he must have set it off, because it shot into the sky with a whoosh. He stared up at the clouds and waited until it parachuted back down into the grass.

Lana didn't notice him at first. She was looking at her feet. "Oh my god, gross. Nachos crapped on my shoe." She put my tortoise down and then started wiping her white canvas shoe on the grass.

"That's Salsa, not Nachos!"

"I'm so tired of carrying your turtles around."

Evan noticed Lana leaping around in the grass like her foot was on fire and came over. She kind of blushed and stopped her dramatic act. I carefully set Nachos down in the grass. Tortoises don't smile or anything, but I can tell they're in a happy mood by the way they bob their heads: slow and careful, checking out each blade.

Evan put down his rocket stuff, then squatted to scratch the tortoises. He always says hello to them, and I like that. When he looked up at us, I noticed that his eyes are the exact same brownish yellow as Salsa's shell, which is a bit darker than Nachos'. Evan, for all his space geekiness, wasn't half bad looking, and while I didn't like him that way, I could tell that Lana was starting to act weird around him and that was annoying. Why couldn't she go like someone else rather than making all three of us uncomfortable?

"What's wrong with Nachos?" Evan asked, pointing at her shell.

A new, tiny crack on Nachos' shell didn't look too serious to me. "She probably bumped into something. Don't worry. Nachos is tough."

"There's no small injuries with animals," Evan said. "It could get infected. Maybe you should separate them, just in case, so Salsa doesn't get sick too."

Lana nodded. "Nachos could sure use a break from Salsa."

"What? No. They don't fight like male tortoises," I said.

She ignored me and turned to Evan, pointing to her shoe. "Don't get sucked into carrying one for her like I did. They'll spoil your new shoes. Totally gross."

"Maybe Anna needs something for them to travel in," Evan said.

"That's a good idea," agreed Lana. "Then she could do this on her own."

I glared at Lana. I didn't want to do this alone. I wanted to do this with her.

"I could help," Evan offered. Now, that wasn't so bad. Evan would make an okay tortoise transporter, provided he'd shut up about the solar system. "We have an old plastic wagon," he added. "You could borrow it. Probably even keep it. Wait here. I'll be right back."

"That's okay," I said. "Lana and I like walking them."

But Evan was already jogging back toward his house.

"Did you see the scars on his leg?" Lana said. "And that smashed up bike trailer by the garbage cans in his driveway? Do you think he still rides his bike?"

"I don't know. He won't talk about it," I said, distracted by some lost pet signs taped to the garbage bin. I got closer to see if anyone had lost a tortoise. When I was little, I worried that a ship full of pirates with a big soup bowl might steal Nachos and Salsa, so I refused to go on a cruise holiday. But these fading posters showed missing cats. Probably all of them made a tasty coyote lunch. There was a missing dog too, kind of a chubby little white thing. That sign looked newer. And there was a budgie bird named Blue Boy. It would be much easier to lose a bird than a tortoise, unless the bird was riding on the back of a tortoise like a slow-moving getaway car.

Soon Evan came out of the gate to his backyard. He was pulling a chunky plastic red wagon that was dirty and had old leaves stuck to it. It was exactly the kind of wagon little kids pull up and down a driveway.

"That's so sweet of you," Lana gushed. "Look, Anna, it even has little seatbelts."

I glared at her. "How do you put a seatbelt on a tortoise?"

"You don't need to use the seatbelts," Evan said. "The seat backs go down so it's flat." He shoved each one down with a thud and it looked like a normal wagon.

"Let's try it," said Lana.

Nachos and Salsa barely fit in the wagon, even with the way Evan had set it up. The sides weren't very tall, and I was a little worried the tortoises might fall out if I hit a bump. The plastic tires made a grinding noise on the pavement and the wagon pulled to the left. But Evan was so excited about it, and Lana so pushy, I couldn't really say anything other than: "Thanks, Evan, see you later."

As soon I started pulling the wagon home, I felt like a ridiculous little kid pulling her stuffed animals. Lana was even walking ahead, as if she was trying to avoid being seen with me. Like she was practising for exactly what she was going to do on the first day of middle school.

Lana spun around: "Can my mom take us to the mall now?"

"But it's summer. You can go to the mall anytime. Why don't we see if she'll take us to Putter's Paradise instead?"

"I can't pick out new clothes at that old minigolf place," said Lana. "Another day, okay?"

We kept walking. A woman whizzed by me on a bike, pedaling steadily up the hill. Suddenly I remembered Evan's advice to keep the two tortoises separated. I stopped to wrestle Nachos out of the wagon. But I had to let go of the wagon to hold her with both hands and it started rolling down the sidewalk. "A little help here, Lana?" I called. But she was so far ahead now that she didn't seem to hear me. I ran down the street and grabbed the wagon with my free hand, awkwardly hugging Nachos in the other.

Lana had finally turned around to check on me. She was walking backwards and waving her hands impatiently. "Hurry up, Anna. I want to get to the mall."

CHAPTER SEVEN

The Graphologist's Approach

In the hallway of the changing room I sat on the floor, my back against one stall, and waited while Lana tried on clothes in the stall across from me. Her mom was somewhere in the front of the store. I could only see Lana's socked feet. Some song I'd heard a thousand times filled the stuffy air. I kept spotting these colourful tiny plastic clips on the carpet. Each had a letter on them: M, S, X, L. I decided they went on the hanger to tell you what size each piece of clothing was and must pop off easily because they were all over the place. I gathered a bunch into a pile. Lana opened the door to her stall and smiled at me. She was wearing a flowing mauve top and slick dark pants.

"What do you think?" she asked, posing like a model.

"I think you haven't even made any money yet, so what's the point of all of this?"

"You're no fun to shop with," Lana said, thumping the door shut again.

The store lady had written "Lana" in curvy letters on a white board attached to the door. I wondered what her writing could tell me about her. I wished I'd brought my handwriting analysis book. I needed more practice. Silently, I started to make a list in my head of people who could be my test subjects. For some reason runny-nosed Maddison from graduation was at the top. Maybe it was because I didn't know her very well and so I didn't have to worry about my feelings getting in the way of my growing graphology skills.

Lana dangled a shirt over the door and said, "I don't want this one. It's more you."

I stood up to take the hanger from her. The shimmery blue material felt soft. It wasn't really me, but for a moment, I wondered if I did own it, would it make any difference with Lana? Mom and Dad never bought me clothes from an expensive store like this and especially wouldn't now with Mom out of work. And I didn't have any money, or a way of making money. Bored, I tossed the shirt on a chair by the big mirror at the end of the hall. I picked up one of the plastic clips and chucked it over the door and into Lana's stall. Nothing happened. I chucked another one. This time Lana let out a little annoyed, "Hey." The third one must have landed in her hair, because after a moment it came flying back over the stall at me. I threw three more over the stall.

"You're so immature," Lana said.

I tried to sound innocent. "What? I'm not doing anything."

I scooped up a handful and tossed them over. This time Lana kind of giggled. "This is embarrassing. You're going to get us kicked out. Besides, I've already decided what I'm going to buy once I get my first paycheque."

Before we left the change room, I took a last look at the shimmery blue shirt I'd flung onto the chair.

That night, Mom got excited when I mentioned calling Maddison and even offered to find her number for me. Mom said she had fond memories of Maddison and I playing together in first grade, and I could use a new friend this summer. I told her not to get too excited because with Maddison allergic to dogs, it was unlikely Lana and I would be able to hang out with her all that much. I just needed a new test subject.

While Mom tracked down Maddison's number, I sat at the kitchen island reading chapter four in my graphology book, which was all about "layout" in handwriting. I'd focused so far on letters, but the way the words and sentences look are just as important, according to the author. I pulled out a list I'd made of people around this summer whose handwriting I could analyze: Dad, Mom, Evan, Maddison. I'd started my list over on one side of the page and then slowly shifted over to the other as it grew longer. Some of the names were bigger and some were smaller. I'd always thought that a neat and tidy list (like the kind Lana would probably make when she's deciding what to buy with all her money) would be a sign of a well-organized person who can make choices quickly. But according to the book, it can mean someone like Lana is an uninspired follower, too stuck on doing things the "right" way and maybe even a little snobbish about how good she is at keeping things tidy. My list style, however, doesn't mean I'm sloppy. It means I'm spontaneous and full of inspiration.

When Mom handed me the phone, I was kind of expecting to hear Maddison sniffling, but she didn't at all.

Before I even got a chance to tell her about graphology, she started to tell me about the sleep-away camp she was going to in the mountains, a camp for kids with serious allergies.

"We get to do archery and canoeing, and everything is peanut free," she said.

I wondered if the camp was in a giant bubble, like the dome over the indoor tennis courts by the middle school, so kids with pollen allergies could go hiking without sneezing. But I didn't say that out loud, because Maddison sounded so excited and really, I was a little jealous. Mom would never let me go to sleep-away camp, even in a bubble dome, because she wasn't letting me out of her sight these days. I told Maddison it sounded really fun, especially without the pesky allergens. Then I told her about my new book.

"I've been studying graphology. That's how someone's handwriting can tell you a lot about them. I was going to ask you if you wanted me to analyze your handwriting."

"I'm leaving for camp tomorrow," said Maddison. "I never heard of graph-o-whatever before. How does it work?"

"You write something in cursive and then I analyze it. Something with lots of letters, like this: 'The quick brown fox jumps over the lazy dog.' That has all the letters of the alphabet."

Maddison repeated the phrase to herself. "The quick brown fox jumps over the lazy dog. Why would a fox jump over a dog? Never mind, I'll try to remember it."

"Hope you have fun at camp," I said. Suddenly, I had a blast of inspiration. I could make money by charging people for handwriting analysis. Maybe I could buy that shimmery blue shirt Lana liked. Or, if not the silly-looking shirt, maybe something else that would help keep Lana close. Maybe I could buy her a signed movie poster from the director of one of those Japanese movies. Or buy an app for Mom's phone so we could chat, instead of her and Harlow Godfrey sending each other smiley face emojis and photos of their cute shoes. So I told Maddison: "If you do want the full handwriting analysis, which really offers the best insight into your abilities and abnormalities, it's five dollars. I only take cash."

"Oh," said Maddison. "Let me think about that. I should go, I've got a lot of packing to do."

When I hung up, I wasn't sure whether to cross Maddison off my list or not. But then I crossed her off, because if I were going to camp, even a camp without allergens, I would be having too much fun to think about scribbling stuff on paper for someone I hardly even knew. I probably wouldn't hear from Maddison again until middle school. And by then she would have forgotten me and would probably be sitting at lunch with her new camp friends, laughing over their peanut-free memories.

CHAPTER EIGHT

Common Challenges Encountered

The next time I went to Lana's house, a dog was jumping up and scratching at her screen door. He had white curls and black-brown eyes. He was a small dog, about the size of a North American desert tortoise. The dog didn't bark, which was disappointing. I had hoped he would be yapping and foaming at the mouth so Lana would change her mind about dog sitting. But when Lana came to the door to let me in, she scooped up the wiggly dog, who licked her hands like crazy.

"Isn't he adorable, Anna?" Lana said, grinning. But she didn't wait for an answer. She started talking to him in the silly voice adults usually uses on babies. "Aren't you adorable, Charlie boy? Aren't you so a-dor-able?"

The screen door slammed shut behind me. "What's that stuff on his chin?" I asked. Yellow crusty stuff hung off his mouth. My hopes lifted. Maybe Charlie had rabies. Then I got a whiff of him. He smelled like a kindergarten kid who spent too much time on the spinny playground equipment on hot dog day.

A woman's voice said, "That's why he can't go on vacation with us." I looked up and saw a woman standing in the front hallway with Lana's mom. I'd never seen her before. She had short purple hair and huge eyes magnified under even bigger glasses. She held a red leash. She looked the opposite of Lana's mom, who always pulled her dark hair back in a ponytail and wore fancy suit jackets.

The purple-haired woman wiped Charlie's chin with the cuff of her sweatshirt. "Charlie gets carsick."

"Gross. Why would anyone want a dog like that?" I asked.

"Don't be rude," Lana said. She gently placed Charlie back on the ground and he darted away, down the hall.

"Your friend does have a point," said the purple-haired woman. "No one seems to want to adopt him. We're fostering him for a shelter. I found him as a stray near here on Fifteenth Street and we've hunted for the owner, but so far no one has claimed him. He's sweet, but he's not a good fit for us. My boyfriend and I like road trips too much."

"Is he a runner? Do we need to worry about him digging his way out of the yard or anything?" asked Lana's mom.

"No, I don't think so. But just in case, the shelter put a chip in him, so if he runs off and someone finds him, they'll get in touch with the shelter, who will get in touch with you."

The dog trotted toward us carrying one of Lana's small stuffed toys in his mouth. The pink mouse had been gutted, with its fluffy white insides dragging along the floor.

Lana gasped. "Charlie!"

"Oh, and keep him away from stuffed toys," said the purple-haired woman, tugging the mouse out of his mouth. "He eviscerates them."

She then started to give instructions to Lana about how to take care of Charlie. Lana's mom made notes on a pad of paper. Charlie zipped around the house exploring, his nails clicking on the hardwood floor. I got impatient and decided that if this dog was going to put a temporary wedge in my friendship with Lana, it was time for me to set my terms.

"I'm not picking up after him when he does his business," I whispered to Lana, pulling her away from the purple-haired lady and her mom, who were now deep into a conversation about the upcoming road trip to the Baja Peninsula. Turns out Lana's mom has lots of opinions on gas prices and authentic Mexican food. "And you're not allowed to feed him at the table when I'm around. That's disgusting."

"No poop, got it," Lana said. "Mom said she'll be taking care of that part."

I noticed Lana hadn't promised that she wouldn't feed the dog at the table. What if I fed my tortoises at the table? Lana would be going on and on about salmonella poisoning. That's a real risk with tortoises. I spend a lot of time washing and sanitizing my hands.

"And he's not allowed in my house." I worried about Charlie hurting Nachos and Salsa. He was small, sure, but that didn't mean there couldn't be trouble. I saw how he gutted that stuffed toy, and my parents were already trying get rid of my tortoises. I didn't need trouble.

"Not you too," said Lana. "Harlow said the same thing. Her brother has allergies so I can't bring him to her place either. This is going to be awful. I'm going to be stuck at home all summer."

But I didn't feel sorry for Lana at all.

During lunch that Saturday it was only me and Dad, and I finally had a chance to explain that graphology is not about math and tried to convince him to let me analyze his handwriting. I suggested my skills were worth $10, but he offered me $2 and I'm not very good at bartering, even if it's for the noble goal of raising enough money to keep Lana from becoming best friends with Harlow Godfrey. The phone rang and Dad answered, then passed it to me. It was Lana.

"You have to do me a huge favour," Lana said. "I need you to watch Charlie. Mom said I can't leave him alone because she thinks he'll chew up the couch cushions. Nobody is home and I made a promise that I *have* to keep."

Dad began to clear away the dishes. I got off the stool and headed to my room so I could pull my handwriting book and a clipboard out of my bedside table drawer. "I can't. Mom would never let me stay alone at your house. And you know Charlie can't come here. He's a danger to my tortoises."

"Just shut your door. It's not a big deal. Please?"

I sighed. "Okay, fine. But only for a short time. And make sure he's gone to the bathroom first."

"No poop. Promise. You're the best. I'm coming straight over with him. Harlow is going to be so happy that we won't miss the movie," Lana said.

She hung up before I could tell her no way.

CHAPTER NINE

Simplifications and Complications

For a tortoise person, Dad didn't seem to mind Charlie. He gave the dog a rub on his pink tummy while I gave Lana my strongest you've-betrayed-me glare. After she'd left, I double-checked my bedroom door. I'd taped a homemade sign saying "Keep Shut" on it. Charlie sniffed underneath it and whimpered a few times, then ran back to Dad when he squeaked a rubber dog toy. Lana had left it with us, along with the leash.

Dad had placed his $2 in coins and the clipboard with a sentence written on it on the kitchen island. I'd asked him to write the one with all the letters about the fox and the dog, but he had written: THE QUICK WHITE DOG JUMPS OVER THE LAZY TORTOISE.

"That's printing," I said. "You have to do it in cursive. And they're *not* lazy."

Dad sat down next to me on the stool. Charlie jumped up on Dad's knees so he tossed the toy across the kitchen floor. "I type all day at work. My hand barely remembers how to write, never mind writing anything fancy."

I knew it! What a waste of time learning cursive was in school. All those hours practising the letters, connecting them, doing that hard S that doesn't look like an S at all. "Why don't you just sign your name? You do that in cursive. I've seen it."

He wrote his full name out just like I'd asked.

Charlie brought back the toy. Dad leaned down and started playing tug-of-war with him. I cracked open the book and began comparing the letters to the pictures inside. But Dad wasn't taking it seriously. He kept squeaking the toy and I could barely concentrate. So I didn't take it seriously either. I explained to him that his signature showed he was extremely frugal with his money and unable to concentrate on the task at hand.

"When do you get to the part about my future?" he said, finally pulling the toy out of Charlie's mouth and chucking it again.

"What do mean?"

"The fortune telling part. Like when I'm going to finally get my helicopter licence and when will my kid qualify for the World Cup? Will I be featured on the news after I finally climb Mount Everest?"

"Graphology isn't about telling the future," I said with a sigh. "It's about finding out who a person is deep down inside."

"Oh," he said, frowning. "I thought it was like palm reading or tarot cards. A glimpse-into-the-future kind of thing."

"Fine," I said, slipping the coins safely into my pocket. I thought carefully about what I'd say. "You won't get your helicopter licence because you're an accountant and afraid of heights. Your kid won't qualify for the World Cup because she hates soccer, and you are too out-of-shape to climb the stairs at work, never mind Mount Everest. That's all in the way you write your big Ts. See?"

"I'm not sure I like graphology," Dad said.

"No refunds. It says so on page 186," I lied.

Dad didn't want me to analyze his handwriting any further after that. So I took a moment to think about what went wrong. I figured if I was going to cheat at handwriting analysis and tell people the future, I ought to tell them exactly what they wanted to hear, rather than what I thought they needed to hear. That way they'd pay me to do it again, especially if I left unanswered questions, like the exact numbers of their big lottery win. Lana came to mind first, with all that dog sitting money coming in, but then I remembered I had already looked at her handwriting and it hadn't been pretty (not her handwriting, but my analysis of it). Then I thought Evan would be easy because I already know what he wants his future to look like.

Everyone knows.

Unfortunately, Dad made me bring Charlie on the walk to Evan's house later that afternoon. As I clipped on his leash, I thought about Lana's promise that he had already done his business. No dog waste would be in *my* future. Charlie was a real pain to walk because he wanted to stop every ten seconds and pee or sniff things that I figured were covered in other dogs' pee.

As I got closer to Evan's house, I noticed something in the driveway, near the garbage bins. It was the bike trailer that had gotten hit by the car. The blue fabric cover was sun-faded and partially torn. One of the two back wheels was flat and the other lay on the pavement, the spokes sticking out in every direction. Evan had been really lucky that the trailer full of model rockets had been hit, knocking over his bike. The car could just as easily have hit him.

I knocked on the door, the leash in one hand and my clipboard under my other arm. He answered and crouched down to scratch Charlie behind the ear. I explained that I was looking after the dog for Lana.

"Lana's not much of a pet sitter if she's already dumping him on you," he said.

Evan's mom would never let me into the house with a dog, so Evan and I walked across the street to the park instead. We talked under the shade of a big tree, far away from the clumps of lilac bushes that stank with the musty sweet smell of dying flowers. I handed Evan my clipboard. A pencil dangled off a string attached to the metal clip, which held some fresh sheets of lined paper to the board.

"Do I ever have an opportunity for you," I told Evan. "For ten dollars I will tell you your future. All you have to do is write one sentence on this piece of paper. And I mean write in cursive, like the teachers make us do when the class is acting up."

"You're going to predict the future? Based on what I write down here? But I don't have ten dollars on me."

"Do you have any money at home? It's all going to a good cause."

"I'm not interested in this kind of pseudoscience stuff," he said.

"Look, why don't you write something down and then we can go from there? Try this sentence, 'The quick brown fox jumps over the lazy dog.' That has all the letters in the alphabet." I thought I would impress him with that fact.

"It's a pangram," he said.

"No, it's a sentence with all the letters of the alphabet in it," I said.

Evan stared at me for a moment, kind of confused, and then took the clipboard and started writing. He handed the clipboard back to me. At least he had written it in cursive. I noticed that the loops in his letters were tightly closed and his writing slanted way to the right. For a moment, I wished I had my book so I could discover what those features meant, but then I remembered I was going to be making it all up.

He had written: "You can't tell the future by reading this sentence."

I didn't want to let Evan see my irritated expression, so I made a very serious face. I pretended to study the letters carefully by nodding and uh-huhing while moving my fingers along the pencil marks. "I can tell by the way that you slant your letters to the right, as if they are taking flight, that you have a promising future." I paused and squinted my eyes like I was thinking really hard. "And this distance, between the loops here and the lines there, indicate that you are not of this world. You are destined for *another* world." I looked at him to see if he was interested. He brushed his dark hair back out of his eyes and leaned forward to look at his own writing. I continued. "As you can tell, graphology is a science. I've been studying it. If you want to know more about your future, that will be five dollars. That's a deep discount, only for friends."

"Five bucks? So you can tell me that I'm going to space one day?" Evan said.

That took me by surprise. How had he guessed where I

was going with this? I stammered, "If I've helped you foresee your destiny, then you already owe me money."

Evan shook his head. "I have no idea what gra-what-ever-ology is, but I doubt it's a science. Sounds more like loopy nonsense to me. And I don't want to be an astronaut anymore. That's just a stupid thing little kids say. I'm not giving you any money. And I want that wagon I gave you for Nachos and Salsa back."

A part of me felt disappointed Evan didn't want to be an astronaut anymore. It was fun when we were little to imagine this future with him, jumping between the giant boulders on the playground, pretending they were moon rocks and that gravity would never pull us back onto the ground. He looked upset with me, and a little sad, like I ripped off his favourite Star Wars band-aid. Suddenly, I was worried that I didn't know Evan as well as I thought I did. I glanced over at the wrecked bike trailer.

"You've changed since that car hit you."

Evan glared at me. And I suddenly worried that I had brought up something I wasn't supposed to bring up. He hadn't talked to me at all about the accident. I'd heard all the details from my mom, who'd heard it from his mom. The scrapes and bruises were mostly healed, except for those scars on his leg. So what was the big deal? Now Evan started to walk away from me.

I shouted after him, waving the clipboard. "No, wait. I did it wrong. You're right, I can't predict the future. But I can take this home and analyze it properly. I can tell you who you really are."

He stopped in the middle of the road and turned around. "You're not that insightful, Anna."

"I am too," I shouted back at him. "How's this for insight: You are helping ruin my friendship with Lana. If she didn't act so stupid and goofy around you then things wouldn't be changing. She wouldn't need people like Harlow around to tell her how to dress and act to impress boys like you."

I was expecting that would really shake him up, maybe he'd apologize. But he kept walking back to his house. "You can keep that stupid wagon," he shouted, not even turning around.

I tore Evan's handwriting sample off the clipboard, folded it up and stuffed it in my pocket. I would put it with Lana's contract in my bedside drawer. This handwriting analysis business wasn't going very well. If I were still in elementary school, I could probably drum up a few gullible clients in the younger grades. Or if lived about a hundred years ago, I could probably sell my skills to people wanting to sift through handwritten job applications or the diaries of suspected criminals. I needed to come up with a new way of making some money.

I tossed the clipboard into the park's garbage bin. Then, as I was walking through the grass towards home, I felt Charlie tug at the leash. He was turning and then he squatted down and did exactly the thing Lana promised he wouldn't do.

CHAPTER TEN

The Writer's Degree of Attention

I have dealt with lots of tortoise droppings in my life. Because they are so small and pleasant, I usually don't bother digging them out of the grass. It's like all-natural lawn fertilizer. Doggy waste is entirely different. You must pick it up. It's the law or something. I glanced around, hoping no one had seen Charlie squat down and do his business, but there was Mom's favourite snoopy old lady, on her knees by a flower patch in her front yard, staring right at me. Mrs. DeJong. She waved at me with her spade. I took a deep breath and walked back to the park's garbage bin, where somebody, probably Mrs. DeJong, had hung a plastic grocery bag stuffed with more bags. I took one out and then returned to the spot with the mess. Pinching my nose, I squatted down and reached out with my free hand to pick it up with the bag. But I couldn't do it. I just couldn't. I spotted a nearby rock and picked that up instead. I stood up again, dragged Charlie back to the garbage bin and threw out the plastic bag with the rock in it. Done. But Mrs. DeJong was already crossing the street, smiling at me. Charlie started leaping about on his leash, whimpering.

"And who's this?" she said in her faintly Dutch accent, reaching down to pet him. "Is this the dog your friend is looking after? Your mother told me all about him."

"Yep. This is Charlie." I watched her scratching him under his curly white chin. She had long fingers and dirt under her nails. Her hand was wrinkled and lined with blue veins. I realized Mrs. DeJong was probably a fantastic hand-writer. She probably spent her days in a one-room schoolhouse back in Amsterdam writing in cursive over and over on a little black chalkboard because no one had invented the keyboard. And she was also probably rich, because she lived alone and had no one to spend her money on. "Do you know about graphology, Mrs. DeJong? It's the study of handwriting. I'm an expert at it and I'm only charging $5. I can analyze your handwriting and tell you your future."

"That's a funny thing for a child to be doing these days," she said, standing back up again and staring straight at me. "I'm too old to want to learn anything about my future. However, I do have a job for a girl who's responsible like you and knows to pick up after a dog."

I felt a twinge of guilt, but I nodded.

"I don't understand how people could be so careless." She started walking, her head bent over, staring into the grass. "I will pay you $1 for every mess you pick up in this park. Once you're done, come tell me how much I owe you. I'll trust you to be honest. You can do this job as often as need be. Just keep this park nice and clean."

My stomach turned a little but then I thought about how poorly my handwriting analysis business had been going. My future might be in sanitation. Maybe neighbours with dogs would pay me to clean their yards. I could charge by the mess, or if I had a scale, by weight. Unappealing? Yes! But that's why people would pay me, just like Lana and her doggy sitting.

"I'll do it!" I said.

Mrs. DeJong walked right over to where I had left Charlie's droppings and shook her head. "Of course, I won't pay you for this little dog's mess."

I could feel my face turning hot. My future as a scooper was at risk, so I rushed over to the plastic bag full of bags and fished one out. I was already imagining all the ways I could clean up dog doody without actually touching it. I could try a shovel, maybe, or those pincher grabber things that I got for Christmas when I was eight. But I knew I had to pick up Charlie's mess now and in front of Mrs. DeJong. It was like an audition for the starring role in a play. I smiled at her then walked back over to the spot. I crouched down and gagged a little on the stink, which mixed with the dying lilacs to create a particularly unfortunate stench. I turned the bag inside out and kind of slid it over my hand like a glove. Then I reached down, grimaced, and grabbed the warm, soft lumps through the bag. I flipped the bag inside out again. None got on my hands. I tied a knot, walked back to the garbage, and tossed it. Mrs. DeJong nodded approvingly and I knew I had gotten the part.

As I walked Charlie over to Lana's house, excited about my new career path, I promised myself not to tell Lana yet. I was still mad at her for dumping Charlie on me so she could hang out with Harlow Godfrey and I figured if she knew it had actually all worked out for me, then she wouldn't feel guilty enough.

When Lana answered the door, Charlie jumped on her and wagged his tail like crazy. I was about to explain to Lana what a bad friend she'd been when she suddenly apologized. "I didn't mean to do that to you, Anna. I got so excited to see that anime movie and didn't really think. Why don't we go to the pool on Friday for the pre-teen swim? I'll have to find someone who can watch Charlie. My mom says she has to go into work for a meeting."

That made me forget all about why I was mad at Lana. Last summer, my mom took us to the pool on hot days. We'd wait until the pool was nicely crowded with kids and she was sprawled out on a deck chair and really into her book before we'd do all the things we weren't supposed to do, like cannonballs off the diving board and going down the twisty slide headfirst. Even if it wasn't Putter's Paradise, the pool was way better than the mall. This summer we were finally old enough for the pre-teen swim. And that meant no moms allowed.

I handed Lana the leash. "My mom won't let me go to the pool alone. At least your mom has work. Hovering over me is my mom's new full-time job."

"What if your mom had someone else to hover over that day?" Lana said with a smirk.

We both stared down at Charlie, who was tangling himself in his leash in a pointless attempt to catch his tail.

"My mom could watch Charlie," I said. "It's the perfect distraction."

At home, I found Dad in my room, kneeling on the carpet and looking silly in orange rubber gloves. Mom was still out. Salsa was already in an old plastic kiddy pool Dad had dragged out of the shed. I quickly scooped up Nachos and put her in the pool too so Dad wouldn't notice the tiny crack on her shell. I'd forgotten Evan's advice to separate them. Dad cleaned the habitat while I explained about how I was going to make a bucket of money as a dog waste scooper. When he was done, he sighed, stood up and peeled off the rubber gloves. Then he took me into the kitchen and pulled his tablet out of his briefcase.

"I want to talk to you more about Nachos and Salsa's future," he said, sitting down on a stool at the island. "My old roommate sent me photos of his farm. Look at how nice it looks."

"Put that away," I said, ignoring a glimpse of a red barn against a blue sky. "Nachos and Salsa aren't going anywhere."

"Anna, the responsible thing to do is give the tortoises a home for life. They are still young, relatively speaking. They both ended up in my care accidentally and I never intended to keep them this long. The plan was to give them back. It just took Frank a lot longer than we thought to get his life on track. You're just a kid and you can't be expected to look after them properly. Your mom and I need to make an adult decision on your behalf."

"Frank dumped them and went to India! This is their home now." I was so sick of being called a kid. "Why are you siding with Mom all of a sudden? Don't you care about Nachos and Salsa?"

At that moment, I heard the door open. Mom came

into the kitchen carrying bags full of groceries. "What's all the noise about?"

My eyes felt swollen with tears but seeing her made me remember that I wouldn't be able to go to the pool with Lana unless she agreed to let us go alone. I wiped my nose with my sleeve and took a deep breath.

"We're talking about the tortoises," Dad said. "Let's just meet my old roommate, Anna. His farm is not far out of town. If you think it's the right place, you could always visit them whenever you want."

"No way."

I turned my back on him and looked at Mom. "Can Lana and I go to the pool on Friday? It's pre-teen swim."

"Alone at the pool? You girls would need a parent to supervise you," Mom said.

"But you can't come. That's the rule for pre-teen swim. Besides, Lana needs someone to watch the dog and we were hoping you could do it."

Mom put the bags on the counter and pulled out an egg carton. "Isn't that Lana's job?"

"It's only for a few hours. Please? You can drop us off and pick us up."

"I'm not sure you two are mature enough to be at the pool on your own. And I'm not sure I want to look after a dog."

"What about the tortoises, Anna?" Dad said. I looked at him and looked at Mom. It felt like somehow, if I said no to Dad, Mom would say no to me. That's how they worked. But I knew Dad liked Nachos and Salsa. Wasn't he just cleaning their habitat? I still had a chance.

"Okay, I'll meet your old roommate," I said. "You'll see how wrong this is."

Mom smiled at me. "That's a good first step, Anna. I guess if Lana needs someone to watch the dog, I'm happy to help. But only this one time. Maybe Charlie and I can even keep an eye on you both from outside of the chain-link fence."

"Mom, that would be so embarrassing." I gave Dad a pleading look.

Dad intentionally tapped on the tablet that held the photos of the farm, sending me a little reminder of my latest promise. "Mom's kidding," he said. "I'm sure you and Lana will be fine on your own."

CHAPTER ELEVEN

Common Misconceptions Facing the Graphologist

Lana showed up at the park lugging a beach bag with little hearts on it. She wore new sunglasses and had Charlie on a leash. Any chance he got, he licked her all over her ankles, which is another reason why tortoises are better than dogs. Mom promised to pick us up at the park by our house after Charlie had gotten some exercise. I didn't mind, because it gave me a chance to make a little spending money for the pool trip. But when Lana saw me pick the dog waste out of the grass, she twisted up her face.

"Eww, why are you doing that?"

"Mrs. DeJong pays me to clean up the park," I said as I hunted through the grass for some more brown gold. The sun shone bright. I wished I had sunglasses too.

"You're working as a pooper scooper?"

"It's a better-paying job than yours," I pointed out as I picked up another mess. "I make about a buck every minute. If you do the math, that's $60 an hour. Way more than you make hourly doggy sitting."

I knew that wasn't exactly true. There really wasn't an hour's worth of work in the grass, but Lana was too grossed out to do the math.

Mom, when she'd found out about my new business idea, had called me a young entrepreneur and decided to supervise me while teaching me all about self-promotion. She kind of went overboard, designing and printing off business cards and dropping them off in the neighbours' mailboxes. But Mrs. DeJong was still my only client. Mom said maybe we needed to do more market research. I thought she needed her own job.

I held up the full, sagging baggy for Lana. "See? Now I can buy you chips at the pool."

"I've got my own money," Lana said, squishing up her face in disgust.

I walked over to the garbage bin with the posters for lost pets on it. The bird poster was gone, but a few sorry cats and a dog remained. Lana followed me with Charlie trotting behind her.

"What's that sign about?" Lana asked, pointing at the dog.

"It's just a lost dog. It's been there for ages."

"He looks a little like Charlie," said Lana. "Charlie was a stray. What if it's him?"

"It's not him. That dog's too fat. They are probably the same breed. Dogs of the same breed all look the same."

I heard a honk and looked up to see Mom pulling up in the minivan. I tossed the baggy. Suddenly I remembered that Charlie got carsick. I hadn't warned Mom about that one. Maybe Lana had a towel with little hearts on it that matched her beach bag. We could use it to mop up the vomit.

"Tell my mom to wait a minute," I said. "I've got to get my money from Mrs. DeJong."

Peering through the chain-link fence around the pool, I could see a blue rectangle stuffed with screaming boys and stuck-up girls, all around our age. We waited in a long line to get in, baking in the hot sun. Finally, inside the damp coolness of the girls' change room, we opened about a million lockers until we found an empty one to share. We both had our swimsuits on under our clothes. Lana had a fancy new bikini with hearts to match her beach bag and I still had my tankini that was all faded from last summer. But I didn't really care. I couldn't wait to have a perfect Anna and Lana afternoon in the cold water. I didn't even worry about how upset my mom would be when Charlie puked on the minivan carpet. I snapped my purple goggles on.

Lana smiled. "You look silly."

"My eyes get all red and itchy without them."

We stepped around the puddles on the tile floor and headed for the showers.

"Let's see if we can get the fancy lounge chairs," Lana said.

"I don't need a chair. It's so hot out there. I'm not getting out of that pool."

The shower water was cool and refreshing, but Lana refused to go under. "My hair will get wet."

"We're going swimming," I pointed out.

But when we stepped out onto the burning concrete on the pool deck, I learned that Lana had no intention of going swimming at all. She pushed her way through the crowd to an empty lounge chair, laid her towel flat, and sat on top of it. "This is perfect! You'll have to find another one and drag it over here, Anna."

"What? No, let's go in the water first." I tossed my towel at her. "It's too hot to sit out here."

Lana shoved my towel to her feet, put on her sunglasses and leaned back. "Maybe later."

I turned around, took a deep breath, and tried not to let Lana get to me. But my deep breath wasn't working. So I took an even deeper breath and then made a running cannonball into the pool, hoping that Lana would get a little of my splash on her new swimsuit. As I sunk down into the icy water, everything was muffled, and I could see my own bubbles and other people's arms and legs. I tried to sink to the painted blue bottom but I was running out of breath, so I swam to the surface and popped back up into the blurry noise of the crowded pool. I turned around, hoping to see Lana soaking wet and upset, but she was talking to Harlow Godfrey, whose stupid palatal expander was glimmering in the sunlight. Lana and Harlow. It felt worse than pool water up my nose. I swam in the other direction, bumping into elbows and shoulders along the way. If Lana wasn't going swimming, then I was going to pretend it didn't bother me. I'd go headfirst down the slide without her. But after a while of pretending I was having fun by myself, I felt shivery and bored. I hauled myself out and dripped my way back to Lana, who was pretend-sleeping under her new sunglasses. Harlow Godfrey had pulled up a lounge chair next to her and was also fake sleeping. I grabbed my towel and wrapped it around my tankini and sat down in an empty plastic chair next to Lana. "Let's go home."

Lana sat up and pushed her sunglasses up into her hair. "But we only just got here."

Harlow Godfrey glanced over at me, but I couldn't see her eyes through the mirror of her sunglasses. "Oh, hey, Anna. Nice goggles. I didn't know you were going to be here too."

"Yeah, well, you're hard to miss." Too tall, mouth too shiny. I didn't say that part out loud though.

"We were planning which movies to watch for the Miyazaki marathon," said Lana. She turned to Harlow. "Anna doesn't get Japanese anime, so there's no point asking her opinion."

"But *Spirited Away* is a classic. How could anyone not like it?" said Harlow.

I glared at her. "I guess you've never noticed that the characters' weird black mouths flap around in a way that doesn't even match what they are saying."

"That's because the original voices were in Japanese," Harlow said, sounding frustrated. "It's dubbed over in English. It won't always match."

I leaned over and hissed into Lana's ear. "You're ignoring me."

Lana frowned slightly. "I'm enjoying the sun. You're being too sensitive. Want to get us salt and vinegar chips?"

"No." I folded my arms and listened as they talked about movies. I felt ignored and annoyed with Lana. Hadn't I been trying to make this friendship work? Lana had manipulated me into going to the pool, lounged around like she was oh-so-important, had ambitions to be Harlow Godfrey's best friend and then called *me* the sensitive one? Maybe her handwriting analysis *was* accurate.

"I'm calling my mom to pick us up. Give me the locker key."

Lana unhooked the key from her perfectly dry towel and scowled at me. "Geez, you're being such a baby."

I stood up and purposely shook my hair so droplets would spray over both of them. While they were frowning and wiping off their sunglasses, I stomped back to the change room, fighting the urge to push all the short boys bumping into me right into the pool.

During the drive home, Mom proved once again how oblivious she was to my moods by insisting on cheerfully going on and on about Charlie. She'd left the dog at home with Dad. The van smelled suspiciously like doggy puke and carpet cleaner, but Mom didn't even bring it up.

"Does Charlie have any sweaters, Lana?" Mom asked. "He looks like he would get cold in the winter. I could knit him one up in no time."

I felt my anger bubbling up. "Dressing animals up in human clothes is dumb."

"Are you forgetting Salsa and Nachos' wedding?" Mom said.

Okay, so I dressed them up like a bride and groom once, but I was four.

Mom looked at Lana through the rearview mirror. "You and Charlie are staying for pizza, Lana. I won't take no for an answer."

I gasped. "Does that dog really need to be in our house all evening? Dad better be watching him closely right now. He could really hurt Nachos and Salsa."

"Just keep him out of your bedroom," Lana said to me. "What's the big deal?"

"You saw him with your stuffed mouse. He could tear my tortoises apart," I said.

She turned to look out the window, leaving me staring at her perfectly dry hair.

At my house, Lana sat down on the floor with Charlie and rubbed his tummy, cooing and going on and on in baby talk to him. It was like she didn't even realize how much more attention she gave that dog in ten minutes than she had ever given Nachos and Salsa. I watched her for a moment, then went to my room to get the graphology book from my bedside table drawer. I made sure to shut the bedroom door tight so Charlie wouldn't get in. I went back into the living room and held up the book.

"Remember how I found this old book on handwriting analysis at school? Well, I thought I'd try it out on you before anyone else. I analyzed your writing."

Lana gave Charlie one last smooch and stood up. "I thought I told you I didn't want to be your science experiment."

"Well, it's done now. I used the contract we wrote up. Aren't you curious?"

She frowned but said, "A little."

I pulled out the slip of folded paper with her results, but then held it away from her grasp. "I'm warning you now that it's not me who comes up with the results. It's all in the book."

"Why? Is it bad?" Lana looked worried. I handed the paper to her and she started reading it. I could see her expression kind of droop. "Is this what you think I am? Manipulative and self-important?"

I held up the book. "That's just what it says based on

the way you write your letters. It's all in here. It told me you're ambitious too, but in the bad way. Like people who make YouTube videos of themselves curling their hair and expect to be famous."

Lana's eyes got all watery. "You're the one who made me write that stupid contract, Anna. And you're the one who gave me this dumb analysis to read because you're jealous about Harlow."

"You're being too sensitive, just like it says there."

"I'm taking Charlie home. Tell your mom I wasn't hungry."

"You've got it all wrong. I'm a graphologist. I'm a professional. I tell you what your handwriting says about you."

Lana was already at the door, swinging her beach bag over her shoulder. She called to Charlie and clipped his leash on him. Then she put her sunglasses on and said: "You need to grow up."

I'd wanted her to feel hurt, but I hadn't expected that I'd feel so hurt too.

During dinner, all Mom wanted to talk about was stupid Charlie. She seemed more disappointed that the dog had left than she was about Lana storming out on me. Afterwards, I slammed the door to my room. I wanted to be alone. I went over to check on Nachos. She crawled up to the edge of the habitat to get a shell scratch. Her damaged spot was looking a little worse—the scute had turned whitish and dimpled.

Nachos looked up at me. Poor girl. She needed to see the vet.

"But if I tell my parents I let you get sick, they will give you away to that Frank guy for sure," I whispered. I wished for a moment that Lana wasn't so mad at me. She was good at fixing things. Not just pencil sharpeners. Even big problems like this one. Together we could figure out how to help Nachos.

"Maybe I can take you to the vet on my own," I said.

It wasn't such a crazy idea. Dad had asked me to book a checkup appointment, it was just a matter of making it for when Mom and Dad were both busy. The vet wasn't that far away, but it was much too far to walk, especially carrying a sick tortoise. I needed a tortoise transporter. Suddenly I remembered the wrecked bike trailer in Evan's driveway. I could drag that home and fix it up. Nachos and Salsa could ride in the back and I could cycle to vet. With a bike trailer, I would show my parents that I was a responsible pet owner who takes care of her tortoises. I wouldn't even miss Lana's steady, tortoise-carrying hands. Harlow Godfrey could have her friendship; I wouldn't need it anymore.

CHAPTER TWELVE

Deviations and Peculiarities

On Sunday morning Dad reminded me about our appointment with his old roommate to see his farm. We drove outside the city and passed lots of farmers' fields. My dad likes to moo as we drive by cows, which is a habit you'd think he'd have outgrown by now. At a turnoff onto a dirt road, a huge scarecrow hung out by the ditch, forever chewing on the same piece of hay. We passed a sign for a petting zoo. I liked places like that once. What little kid doesn't like a petting farm? Brushing friendly goats. Patting grass-munching ponies. Fleeing from crazed peacocks determined to snatch a sandwich out of your hands.

But when the road ended and we passed a set of gates, I realized that the petting zoo *was* the old roommate's farm. I panicked. The small parking lot was full. Parents fussed over little kids who rubbed slimy noses with their sleeves and threw hats out of strollers. All those grimy little hands could be touching my tortoises' shells and force-feeding them Goldfish crackers and Cheerios.

"I'm not getting out of the car," I said.

Dad took off his seatbelt. "Okay, so this isn't quite what we expected. But if the tortoises lived here, you could visit anytime."

"I don't want to visit them. Our house is their home."

"Let's just check it out, okay? We drove all the way out here. He's expecting me."

I yanked off my seatbelt and pushed open the car door, stepping onto the gravel. "Only if we're quick," I said, slamming the door.

Dad's old roommate wore a checkered bandana around his neck and had a black moustache that bounced up and down while he talked. Dad shook his hand and they spent a few moments catching up beside a pen that swarmed with kittens and about a hundred kids trying to scoop them up. I thought a kitten might get stepped on or strangled, but Frank didn't seem bothered. He kept glancing over at a horse that was standing by a fence.

The red barn behind the horse looked exactly like the ones in cartoons. Something about it seemed fake, like it was cut out of a picture book about Old MacDonald's Farm and pasted on a blue cardboard sky. The whole place smelled like straw and manure, and the kids shrieked so much that I wished I'd brought earplugs. One kid nearby was bawling because a goat had not only eaten all the pellets his mom had bought him, but the paper cup the pellets came in too.

Frank seemed really interested in Nachos and Salsa. "I've been missing those old gals. And they'd be a real hit with the kiddos."

"Can you show me where you'd keep them?" I asked. "What kind of habitat you would have for them?"

"I hadn't given it much thought. I'm sure we'd make do. We could put them near the pond."

"They're tortoises," I said. "They'd drown!"

Dad furrowed his brow. "Would the kids go into the habitat? Like with the kittens?" he asked.

I pictured a two-year-old trying to sit on Nachos like he was a stool. My dad never let me do that, and now that I'm older I understand why.

"It's a petting farm. We generally let the kids in all the pens. Well, except for the one with that horse."

I looked over. A little boy in a baseball cap reached up to pat the horse on its muzzle. It was a brown horse, not too big, and it was shaking its mane. Frank shouted over to the kid to stop. Suddenly the kid screamed. The horse was munching on his hand. "Excuse me a second," said Frank. As he ran over, the kid managed to get his hand out of the horse's mouth. Frank gave the mom a real talking to, constantly stabbing his finger on a sign that read "Don't feed the horse."

I turned to Dad. "Now do you believe me? This isn't right."

"Looking back on my college days, maybe I did all the work when it came to the tortoises," Dad said. "But Frank's a good guy. He just needs a reminder about the dos and don'ts of taking care of tortoises."

"What he *needs* is a reminder about the dos and don'ts of running a petting farm," I replied.

When we got home, I heard loud music coming from the living room. Mom sat on the couch knitting, with a big ball of multi-coloured yard at her feet. Her curls were all piled up on the top of her head in an exploding bun. Her phone was on the coffee table, thumping away. She reached over and turned the music down.

"How did it go?" she asked.

"Frank's offer is still on the table," said Dad. He pointed at the knitting hanging off her needles. "What's that?"

She held up a rectangle of knitted fabric. "It's a sweater for Charlie."

I frowned. "Why are you making a sweater for Lana's dog?"

Dad looked at Mom. "Should we tell her about the adoption?"

For a moment, I thought they were going to tell me I was adopted. I had a dizzy feeling, like everything was a lie, that maybe I was really a child born in a llama barn on the frozen tips of the Himalayan mountains. Or maybe I was set adrift in a dinghy in the Pacific Ocean as a toddler and rescued by a kindhearted oceanic exploration team. Which were both cool new backstories. Then I realized that I was being silly, that obviously, just from looking at them, Mom and Dad were my real parents. I have Mom's dark unruly hair and Dad's unfortunately large feet. What they must have meant is they were turning to adoption for their second kid. But I really didn't want another kid to move into our house, especially not one raised in a llama barn or rejected by globe-trotting sailors.

"I like being an only child," I said. "Besides, Nachos and Salsa are like my sisters. That's how I treat them, anyway."

Dad fiddled with his keys. "Well, to put it diplomatically, you haven't shown much of an improvement in your tortoise care routine."

"Actually, honey," my mom said. I hate when she calls me honey—that always means I'm not going to like what she is going to say. "You know how attached I've become to Charlie? He's a rescue dog without a permanent home. And with me having all this free time while I look for a new job—it seems like an ideal moment to fold him into our family."

"Adopt Charlie?" I looked at my dad. He was staring at the ceiling. "But a dog could hurt a tortoise. You're always warning me about that, Dad, whenever I take them to the park."

He looked down at me and forced a smile. "If this is what your mom wants, I'm okay with it. It's been a difficult few months for her. And this wouldn't be some strange dog in the park, it would be Charlie. He's been fine with the tortoises so far."

I kicked a stray ball of red yarn across the living room floor and watched it unravel. "But I don't want a dog. It's not safe for Nachos and Salsa. Charlie guts stuffed animals. And he drools and sheds and jumps up on people. Tortoises don't do any of those things. It's the stupidest idea I've even heard."

"Anna, you're being melodramatic," Dad said. "And please pick up that yarn."

"Give her some time to get used to the idea," Mom said to him. "I wouldn't want to steal Lana's summer job away from her."

Lana! Hearing her name made me even madder. This was all her fault. If she hadn't been trying to dump Charlie on my mom so she could spend more time with Harlow Godfrey, none of this would have happened. I glared at

Mom and then picked up her phone without even asking if I could use it.

"I need to be alone."

I dialed Lana's number as I stomped down the hall into my room. I slammed the door shut. It was dark in the room and smelled kind of funky. I flipped on my lamp and thumped onto my unmade bed, kicking the rumpled bedspread onto the floor.

"Hello?" It was Lana's voice.

"Charlie is your job. He's your dog to deal with."

"Anna, stop. Just stop. I should have told you Harlow was going to be at the pool. But you don't understand—"

"Oh, I understand. I know exactly what you are like."

"What, because you think you can 'read' my handwriting? That's not real. It's made up."

"Because I've known you forever!" I knew I sounded kind of hysterical, but I couldn't stop myself.

"People change, Anna," she said. "You can't look at some scribbles on a piece of paper and try to figure people out. Look, we can still be friends even with Harlow around. And don't get all worked up about Charlie. He's not a bad dog."

"Graphology is real," I said. "You just don't like what it says about you. Anyway, I don't want anything more to do with you. And I don't want anything to do with Charlie."

"You aren't even trying to understand me, Anna. This isn't my—"

But I didn't hear the rest of her sentence because I hung up.

CHAPTER THIRTEEN

Crossing T's and Dotting I's

The biggest obstacle to my plan to convert the trashed bike trailer into an ambulance-like tortoise transporter was Evan. The trailer was in his driveway. And last time I'd seen Evan, I'd not only blamed him for ruining my friendship with Lana, but I'd hinted that he was cheap for refusing to pay me for a handwriting analysis. I decided knocking on the door, rather than calling his house, would give me the best chance of not having to deal with him. His mom would probably answer the door. And she'd give me the trailer without lecturing me on the absurdity of fortune-telling abilities and the probability that Lana had picked out a new best friend all on her own.

As I walked down the street, I pulled Evan's old red wagon behind me so I could return it. It was a not-yet-hot mid-summer morning. Sprinklers sprayed yellowing front lawns, sending water flooding onto the sidewalk. The wagon's thundering wheels got wet, and when I glanced behind me, I could see two dark lines on the pavement. As I neared the park, I started to worry that the bike trailer wouldn't be in Evan's driveway anymore. Maybe someone else had taken it. Maybe some other girl's tortoises were zipping around in it. Maybe the trash collectors had taken it away. It could be in the dump by now.

But the bike trailer was still in the driveway. No one had wanted it. And I remembered why. One of the back wheels lay on the pavement, spokes sticking out everywhere. The other back tire was flat. The blue fabric had turned pale in the sunlight, and it seemed torn in places. I wasn't sure how I would fix it. I knew nothing about bike trailers. Lana was actually good at fixing stuff like this. But now my only hope was Evan, who could at least put together model rockets. I studied his house. The blinds were closed. No one was on the street or in the park. Maybe I could take it without even asking anyone. But I had brought the red wagon and I couldn't pull both home. And if I left the wagon there Evan would figure out who took the trailer. So I decided to knock.

I waited a while and eventually Evan's little brother answered. He came up to my waist, had buzz-cut hair, and was missing about a dozen teeth. The kid saw me and screamed "Evan" about six times down the basement stairs. I tried to shush him and hissed at him to get his mom instead. But Evan came to the door.

"What do you want?" Evan brushed the hair out of his eyes. They had the glassy look of someone who spent too much time in the dark playing video games. He glanced at the red wagon but didn't budge from the doorway. "I don't care if you brought it back. I'm still not interested in your made-up writing guru thing."

"I got another job now. It pays better," I said, leaving out the part about dog messes I was scooping up. "Anyway,

I'm here because I need your old bike trailer. Help me drag it home."

"What do you want that thing for?" he asked.

"For my tortoises," I said.

He looked uncomfortable and scratched at the scar on his leg. "It's trashed."

I remembered that the trailer had been attached to Evan's bike when he'd gotten hit by the car. I felt really stupid, like I'd picked at a scab myself.

"Why don't you ask Lana to help you?" he asked.

"Because I'm not friends with Lana anymore. I know I said that was your fault, but I realize now it's not. And I know you don't like her, not in that way. She's vapid."

"Yeah, but she'd know how to fix the trailer." Evan slipped on his sneakers and led me out onto the driveway. "And I don't think you'll really want it once you smell it."

Suddenly it hit us, kind of an animal stink, but not sharp and burning like that time a skunk sprayed my dad. This smell was different. I stepped back again and plugged my nose. I didn't know what that smell was, but Evan did.

"It's mice, Anna. We've got a whole nest of them in our shed. My mom's not sure what to do. She's mad because they are getting into her garden too." He started to back away, waving his hand in front of his nose. I kind of gagged, but I wasn't going to give up. I could scare the mice out of there. I looked around the yard for a big stick, thinking I could bang on the trailer and frighten the mice out. I wished I hadn't worn flip flops. I found an old hockey stick and pounded on the trailer just the same. It made a satisfying clang against the metal. Nothing scurried over my bare toes. The mice had moved on.

I tossed the hockey stick onto the grass. "See, no more rodents. But it still smells horrible. We can hose it down. You grab the wheel that fell off and I'll drag it back myself."

"That wheel is garbage," he said. He stepped back and folded his arms against his chest. "Besides, you're on your own."

"But I need you. I don't know how to fix anything."

"What makes you think I know how to fix things? I have no idea."

"Who fixed your bike after that car hit it?"

Evan kind of stiffened up. He didn't like to talk about the crash. "No one. I'm not riding my bike anymore. I can walk anywhere I need to go."

"But walking takes forever. It wasn't that bad of an accident. Aren't you supposed to get back on the donkey after you fall off? Or something like that?"

"Horse. And I don't want to talk about this, Anna."

"But you know how to fix a flat tire, right? Just help me and then I can help you with your bike."

"All you do is put air in a flat tire. Anyone can do that." But I could tell he was coming around a little because he picked up the loose wheel with the spokes going everywhere. "This one is going to need more than air."

"I have nine bucks from my new job," I said. "Do you think that's enough for a new wheel? There's got to be videos online that can tell us how to put one on, right?"

"Wheels probably cost more than that."

A long pole stuck out of the front of the trailer. It must attach to a bike somehow. I grabbed hold of it and started to drag the trailer down his driveway. It made a horrible screeching sound as the side without a wheel dragged along the pavement. I tilted it to one side and pulled, but it was heavy and awkward.

"Can I get a little help? Explain to your mom that we're going to take it to my house."

"Okay. But she's going to insist you take something from the garden for Nachos and Salsa. Give me five minutes."

The flat tire thumped-thumped along the sidewalk as we dragged the trailer back up the hill to my house. Evan walked behind me, helping by keeping the trailer tilted on one side while carrying a grocery bag full of greens from the garden. He also held the detached wheel with the spokes going everywhere.

"I saw Lana in the park the other day while I was helping my mom wash her car," Evan said. "I'm not sure she's having so much fun dog sitting anymore."

The mention of Lana kind of squeezed on my heart a little. I looked over my shoulder at him. "Why?"

Evan shrugged. "She was sitting in the grass, staring down into her new phone and the dog was practically on top of her trying to get her attention. But she kept pushing it away. And then it started to run for the street and Lana was screaming at it to come back. My mom had to catch it. I thought it was kind of funny."

"She already has a phone?" Now I felt jealous. "She doesn't even have tortoises destined for internet fame. Salsa could have her own hashtag. Nachos is particularly photogenic."

Evan started to chuckle. I turned around to glare at him and he stopped. "This mice smell is gross," he said. "You're going to have to ask your mom for soap or something. I don't think water is going to make a big difference."

I smiled at him because at that moment, I knew Evan would help me. "And once we get this fixed, we'll fix your bike," I said. "And then I'll help you get back on that donkey."

"It's horse, Anna. You'll help me get back on the horse."

Washing the trailer was the best part because it was a hot afternoon and the mist from the hose cooled us down. Soon it did smell better. I couldn't do anything about the faded colour of the fabric, but I realized the torn parts were vinyl window flaps, so we cut them off. It still had mesh screens and I wasn't going to take Nachos and Salsa biking in the rain anyway. We found a hand pump in the garage and Evan showed me how to pump up the flat tire.

Afterwards, we brought the grocery bag full of lettuce and other leafy green stuff from his mom's garden into my room for the tortoises.

"Nachos," I called. "I've got fresh basil." It was one of her favourites, but Mom said it was too expensive to buy in the store, so Nachos only got it when Evan's mom had extra. I pulled a few leaves out from the bag, the thick smell wafting up, and set them down in front of her. Nachos didn't even bother to move. I gave her a little tickle under the chin. Then I noticed the spot on her shell looked even paler and had even more little dimples.

Evan squatted down to take a closer look at Nachos. "That has definitely gotten worse. When are you going to call that vet of yours? The one with the snakes."

I flinched at the slithery mention. "I haven't made the appointment yet."

"Well, you should at least separate them in case whatever is wrong is contagious," Evan said. "We can use your old paddling pool." It was still in my room from when Dad cleaned the habitat since I'd forgotten to take it back out to the shed.

While Evan set up the pool as a second habitat, I hunted for Mom's phone so I could call the vet. She'd left it on the kitchen island while she folded laundry in the basement. I checked her online calendar. She had one appointment—a job interview—for a Friday morning when Dad was usually at work. Unlike Lana, I don't mind talking to adults, so I called the vet, booked the checkup for that Friday morning, and hung up with a mix of relief that I'd finally made the appointment and worry that I would get caught and my tortoises would be sent to Frank's farm.

"Done," I told Evan once I was back in my room. He'd filled the paddling pool with clean bedding and a water bowl and set up the second lamp. Then he added his garden greens.

I gave Nachos a little pat on the not-gross end of her shell. Then I scooped up Salsa and held her close to my chest. She blinked and slowly stretched her neck, looking left and then right. I figured she was looking for Nachos, but I couldn't risk her getting the gross infection too. So I fished a piece of basil out the bag and let her nibble it instead.

CHAPTER FOURTEEN

Individual Variations

The next morning, I was watching videos about bike repair on Dad's tablet while Mom worked on a rectangle of knitted fabric. She'd stop every so often to wrap it around Charlie, who'd squirm away. It was supposed to look like a doggy sweater, but I thought it looked more like a big fuzzy dishcloth.

Because Mom had offered to adopt Charlie once the foster lady with the purple hair returned from her trip, Lana was taking every opportunity she could to dump him on us. Lana was sneaky about it too, avoiding seeing me by having Mom go over to her place and pick him up. I imagined that free of Charlie, Lana was out doing fun stuff with Harlow Godfrey. Manipulative, self-absorbed Lana. Turned out all that handwriting analysis stuff was eerily accurate.

Mom held up the knitted fabric and frowned. "Do you think it's too big for him?

I shrugged, thinking back to that first week of summer when Mom had offered to knit a tea cozy with me and feeling a twinge regretful that I had turned her down.

"What are your plans for that old bike trailer in the backyard?" she asked.

I'd been prepared for that question. "I thought maybe I'd take Charlie for rides. See if it's easier on his stomach than the car."

"That's so thoughtful of you."

"How's your job hunt going?" I asked.

"I have an interview lined up. It's a part-time job, at least at first. I'd still have lots of time to get the dog settled in," Mom said. "Wait, where did Charlie go?"

"He was right here," I said, looking up from the wheel repair video and searching around the living room.

"Charlie?" Mom called. "Here boy."

"Wait, did I shut my door?" I muttered, tossing the tablet on the couch before Mom had time to answer. I dashed toward the hallway. Charlie was not very big and not very mean, but I remembered how he'd gutted Lana's stuffed mouse and I wasn't sure how he'd react to my tortoises. One scratch or bite could cause a lot of damage, maybe even kill them.

My door was open a crack.

I felt my stomach drop with worry for Nachos and Salsa. I pushed my door wide open. I expected carnage.

But there was Charlie beside Salsa's kiddy pool, stretched out on top my sweatshirt, fast asleep. It was almost like he was protecting her. Salsa was sunning herself under the lamp, not at all worried about the dog. Nachos, in the old habitat with the plants, waddled up to the edge to say hello to me. They really didn't seem to mind Charlie. I gave Nachos a shell scratch and then kneeled down next to the dog. He'd caused a lot of problems for me and Lana, but at least he wasn't interested in hurting my tortoises. I ran my fingers through Charlie's puffy white curls. "I think I'm going to nickname you Cheese. Then it will be Nachos, Salsa, and Cheese."

He opened his big brown eyes and stared up at me. He licked my hand, his tongue rough and wet, then laid his head down again on my sweatshirt.

Mom poked her head around the door. "Everything okay in here? Why is Salsa in the kiddy pool?"

"I was planning on cleaning up the habitat," I lied. "By the way, I made a vet appointment for Friday."

"Finally. I can take you as long as it doesn't conflict with my job interview."

I needed to distract her from the finer details of the appointment. "I should take the dog for a walk," I said.

Charlie looked up at me and thumped his tail.

Mom smiled. "You know, the more I see you taking responsibility with Charlie like this, the more I realize I've been a little hard on you. You might be ready for a new privilege. Your dad and I should talk about you biking to middle school in the fall."

"Really?" I scratched Charlie behind the ear. He wasn't just a somewhat sweet dog. Charlie was an all-access, backstage pass to freedom.

A symphony of lawn mowers and hedge trimmers filled the neighborhood as I walked Charlie down to the empty park. He tugged on the leash a little when a squirrel raced up a pine tree. "Stop it," I told him. "That squirrel would destroy you." While he sniffed around the park and peed, I hunted through the grass looking to make some cash for a new wheel for the trailer. I filled a few bags. While I was tossing them out, I noticed an envelope taped to the bin. It had words written on it: *To the owner of the little white dog.* I wondered if it was from someone who lived near the park wanting to congratulate me on my clean-up abilities. If you didn't know I was getting paid for it, I probably looked like a waste patrol superhero. So I grabbed the letter and tore it open. It was a handwritten note on a white piece of paper.

To the owner of the little white dog,

I'm very sorry to bother you, but your cute little dog looks a lot like my missing boy Yamiska. He disappeared two months ago. Maybe you found him. You can see my sign on this garbage bin. Maybe you've had your dog much longer, but I haven't noticed you around before.

Sincerely,
A sad dog owner

Shocked, I looked around to see if anyone was watching me. No one. I stared at the photo in the missing dog poster and down at poor Charlie, who looked back up at me so innocently. The two dogs were both white and curly, but the dog in the picture was fatter than Charlie, maybe even a lighter shade of cream. Charlie's fur was brownish near the skin. It could be him, if he had lost weight since he went missing and the flash had distorted the colour of this other dog's fur. The missing dog was named Yamiska. Well, if Charlie was the missing dog, he'd answer to that name. Mystery solved. I let go of his leash and started to walk away so I could call him, but he followed me.

"No. Stay," I said. He wouldn't listen. I tried out the name anyway. "Yamiska! Hello, Yamiska." Charlie wiggled his rear and tried to jump up on me. Then I tried his current name. Maybe he likes it more and it's a sign that he belongs with my mom. "Charlie! Hello, Charlie." He did it again—butt wiggling and jumping up. He seemed to like both names just as much. Suddenly I had a thought. In the same sing-song voice I said, "Stinky! Hello, Stinky." He wiggled his rear and tried to jump up on me again. I sighed. Charlie, or whatever his name, wasn't very bright.

I read the letter again, worried about what to do. Charlie, oblivious that his fate hung in the balance, sniffed the grass around us. I needed to talk this letter over with someone, and it couldn't be Mom, not yet anyway. I glanced up at Evan's house. Guaranteed, he was alone in the basement gaming. I tugged Charlie through the park, across the street, and rang the bell.

Evan answered the door, blinking and rubbing his eyes from the blast of sunlight. "Are you here to help me fix my bike?"

I'd forgotten all about that promise. But I didn't have the time now. I held up the letter. "I've got a big problem. Look what I found taped to the trash can when I was picking up after the dogs in the park for Mrs. DeJong. It's about Charlie. Somebody thinks he's their missing dog."

Evan looked at me, confused, and absently scratched his leg scar. "You're scooping poop? Is that the new job you were talking about?"

I waved the letter again. "Evan, focus! There's something unusual going on here." I knew Evan couldn't resist a mystery. He reached out and took it from me, and then read it while I babbled: "What if Yamiska is Charlie? He was a stray after all."

"What do you care, Anna? I thought you didn't want Lana to have a summer job."

He was right. Why did I care? I looked down at Charlie and thought about Mom. The more she poured all her love and caring into Charlie, the less she worried about me. Sure, sometimes I felt a little envious, but job-less Mom was shifting all her worry and smothering onto him, and that was giving me more freedom than ever. If she didn't get to adopt Charlie, she'd probably be so sad she'd be worse than ever, tailing me in her minivan while I biked to middle school. It made me think about those stories of country kids biking happily along gravel roads only to find out they were being tracked by a huge cat, like a cougar or a mountain lion. Then they needed to pedal like crazy to escape. Plus, Charlie wasn't so bad. He'd gotten me a job, even if I wasn't making much money. And he liked Nachos and Salsa.

"My mom is going to adopt Charlie. She really cares about him," I said. "Does the person who lost him even deserve to have him back?"

Charlie was trying to nose his way into Evan's house, so I held him by the collar while Evan got his sandals on. Evan stepped outside, shutting the door behind him. He padded over to the big leafy tree in his front yard and leaned against it, still holding the letter. He liked working things out.

"We know Charlie is a stray. The lady who hired Lana to look after him is his foster family, right? So that means that there's some bigger organization she is volunteering with, like a shelter or something, that takes in strays. If someone lost a dog, wouldn't that be the first place they'd look?"

"Exactly, only a really lazy dog owner wouldn't look in a shelter, or in ads online," I said, joining him in the cool shade of the tree. "And that purple-haired lady told me they put a chip in Charlie so that we could find him if he got lost. You scan him like a turkey at the grocery store and the shelter's name and address pops up. The person who had him before hadn't bothered to put a chip in him. Kind of irresponsible, right?"

I started to imagine a terrible, uncaring owner who really didn't deserve Charlie. My mom, on the other hand, would be a really good dog owner. She'd care about him as much as I cared about Nachos and Salsa.

But then Evan held the letter up and turned the argument around. "They could have been on vacation or in the hospital when Yamiska went missing. Something terrible might have happened, like a car accident. It might not be their fault that he went missing and they couldn't look for him." I started to feel sorry for whoever had lost Yamiska. Maybe it was a girl who really liked him, even though he was a jumpy little mutt, and maybe she had a mom following *her* around in a minivan. I felt torn and didn't know what to do.

Evan wasn't finished. He liked to examine every side of a problem. "What if your dog isn't Yamiska and the person who wrote the letter is completely convinced he is because they miss their own dog so much? Maybe if you respond, you'll create all kinds of problems for Charlie and your Mom."

A crazy ex-dog owner? I hadn't even thought of that. What if they had a thing for tortoises too? "What should I do, Evan?"

"You should ask Mrs. DeJong if she saw anyone put the note on the trash can. She's always watching everything that happens in that park."

"Of course! I can't believe I didn't go to her first."

"Umm, thanks," Evan said. "Can we fix my bike later today?"

"Maybe," I said. But I was lost in my thoughts about Mrs. DeJong. Even if she saw someone hanging around the park, unless she knew that person, all I would have was a description: old or young, man or woman, tall or short. I needed more information. I glanced over at the park, trying to imagine who would tape a letter like this to a trash bin. Then I looked down again at the letter in Evan's hands. It was written by hand in pen. Maybe I could use the graphology book to find out more about the person who wrote the letter. Then I could decide how to handle the problem. But I didn't mention this to Evan because now that we were friends again, I didn't want to remind him of what had upset him in the first place.

CHAPTER FIFTEEN

Form and Degree
of Connection

Mrs. DeJong said she hadn't seen anyone unusual in the park. And she didn't remember anyone coming around regularly with a fat little white dog either. She did have three dollars in park clean-up money for me, so it wasn't a complete waste of time. I walked Charlie home with the letter in my pocket and no more information about who sent it. And the more I thought about trying to analyze the handwriting, the more I heard Evan's words. *Not that insightful. Loopy nonsense.* And it wasn't just Evan. No one believed I could analyze handwriting. I hadn't found a paying client besides Dad, who misunderstood the whole point. And my one freebie, Lana, hadn't appreciated what I had discovered about her.

When I walked Charlie into my house, it smelled kind of like cookies, but not exactly like cookies. Charlie went crazy, yipping and squirming while I tried to unhook his leash from his collar. My mom came to the front entrance wearing oven mitts, and he burst away from me as soon as he could and jumped on her legs.

"Charlie must know that it's for him," Mom said. Then she talked to him in her baby voice. "Can you guess what I'm making for you, Charlie-boo? Can you Charlie-boo?" She smiled at me and talked like a normal person again. "It's dog treats, but shh, don't tell him. It's a surprise for when we adopt him. I'm going to pop them in the freezer once they've cooled."

That strange pang of envy returned, and I had to remind myself that I hadn't wanted to cook anything with her.

I touched the letter in my pocket, unsure if I should pull it out. "I don't know Mom—" But as I walked into the kitchen, there was Maddison sitting at the kitchen island. She had new freckles on her face and about a dozen homemade bracelets sliding down her wrists. Maddison pulled an old tissue out of her pocket and blew her nose.

"Anna!" she finally said, scrunching the tissue into a ball. She handed me an envelope. "This is for you. I forgot to send it from camp."

For someone who has never gotten a letter, I was starting to feel like a post office box. I tore it open and inside I found a lined sheet of paper and five dollars. I unfolded the paper. Maddison had written: *The quick brown fox jumps over the lazy dog.*

Mom glanced over and although she couldn't read it from across the kitchen, she could see that there wasn't much on the page. "That's it, Maddison? You got your dad to drop you off for one sentence? You sure don't have a lot to say."

"But she knows how to follow directions," I said. "Come to my room, Maddison. The dog doesn't usually go in there so maybe you won't sneeze as much."

Inside my room, Salsa waddled up to the edge of the paddling pool and I introduced her to Maddison. Nachos was hiding in her box again. I felt guilty about the damaged spot on her shell, but at least I'd booked the appointment for Friday.

"Why's the other one hiding under that box?"

"She's not feeling so well. How was camp?"

"It was so much fun. I learned how to rock climb and canoe. And we made these bracelets." She held up her arm. Secretly I thought that sounded a lot like a normal camp and not a special camp for allergy sufferers. Maybe her parents got ripped off. "Can I watch you analyze my hand-writing, Anna? I'm curious about how it works."

I glanced at Maddison's sentence again, each letter loopy and slanted to the left. For a moment I pictured her at school and remembered that she was a lefty. I had a sinking feeling that the author of the old handwriting book wasn't too fond of lefties. But I wouldn't let that ruin Maddison's analysis, because she was the only person who believed in my graphology skills.

"It's way easier to do it when the subject of the analysis isn't around. But you can help me with another one. Then I can show you how it's done."

I opened my bedside table drawer and put her letter inside, along with the other scraps of handwriting I'd col-lected, and slid the drawer shut. Just having Maddison interested made me feel like I could find out more about the person who lost Yamiska. I took the mystery letter out of my pocket, unfolded it, and smoothed out the creases. Then I cracked opened *The Guide to Graphology*. It smelled like the farthest corner of the school library, the spot with the beanbag chair. I felt sad for a moment remembering I wouldn't ever be going back to my elementary school. Then Maddison sneezed. What a musty old book.

Maddison read the letter. "Wait. Is this about your Mom's dog?"

"Charlie's not *our* dog. He's a stray. Besides, this is technically an anonymous sample," I explained. "We need to focus on the writing style and not the meaning of the sentences."

I piled up some pillows on the floor and plunked down, my back against the side of my bed. Maddison sat opposite me on her knees, leaning forward to see what I was doing. I stared hard at the letter from "a sad dog owner," trying to forget about the words and their meanings so I could concentrate on the shapes and strokes. The handwriting was over-the-top, much fancier than anything I'd looked at before. Like a little old lady had gulped down a bottle of Coke and a handful of gummy worms before sitting down to whip off a note.

"What are we looking for exactly?" Maddison asked.

I turned to where I'd bookmarked chapter five, and then silently skimmed the first few pages. It talked about how you can learn a lot about someone by how they string together the letters in a word, and even sometimes the words in a sentence.

"See how each letter is connected? That tells you something. Too much connection between the words, and it's almost impossible to read the writing. It means someone is trying to make connections between things that aren't really there."

Apparently, people who do well on crossword puzzles, like Mrs. DeJong, have this kind of writing.

"But if you don't connect all the letters in a word, then you are distracted and have too many ideas in your head. Whoever wrote this letter was not the crossword type. They were more the distracted type. See? Lots of breaks between the big loopy letters, even in the same word."

Maddison nodded. "But what about the letters? Don't they mean anything?"

I flipped ahead to the section on the alphabet in chapter six and decided to focus on one letter to make it easier. I picked M because, according to the author, it's a letter that can be written many different ways so it can tell you a lot about a person. But when we tried to compare the capital M's we noticed they were each different.

I wrote a bunch of words that start with M on a piece of paper. "Look, my M's are basically all the same. Maybe I'm dealing with someone who is crazy, rather than a sad dog owner. I should give up."

"Maybe you need a break," said Maddison, who was flipping through the book. "This book is kind of weird. Look, there's a whole page here about the 'capricious nature' of left-handed writers. I'm a lefty. What does capricious mean?"

"Umm. I think it has something to do with liking pants that stop above your ankles," I lied.

"Capri pants? That doesn't make any sense. Why would my handwriting say anything about my clothing?"

"Graphology is full of insightful surprises," I muttered.

I took the book from her before she read anything else about lefties. What should I do with the mysterious letter? Charlie wasn't even our dog. I needed to give this letter to Lana. She's responsible for the dog. She could deal with it.

My mom called out for Maddison. "Your dad is back from running errands," she shouted.

"I've got to go," Maddison said as she stood up. Her bracelets slid down her arm. "I can't wait to read your analysis of my handwriting. Call me when it's done, okay?"

After she'd left, I found Mom sitting on the end of the couch that gets sunshine from the big picture window, staring into her laptop. Charlie was snuggled up at her feet. Mom glanced up at me.

"You seem thoughtful. Still pondering Maddison's deeply moving letter from camp?"

It was the other note, the mystery one, that I was thinking about, but I wasn't ready to tell Mom yet. Not with all those dog biscuits cooling on the kitchen counter. "It's almost dinnertime," I said. "Lana should be home by now. I'll walk Charlie over to her place for you."

Mom stretched out her foot and gave the dog a rub. He rolled onto his tummy. "That's nice of you to offer to help like that, Anna. You're certainly getting attached to the little guy."

"I need to talk to Lana anyway," I said. "Come on, Charlie, let's go for a walk."

That white fluffball rolled himself back onto his feet and bounded over to me, wagging his tail.

CHAPTER SIXTEEN

The Natural Basis of Personality

After I'd knocked, Lana answered the door. She'd cut her hair shorter and wore a flowing brownish dress. Her new phone was in one hand. Charlie leapt up at her excitedly, digging his claws into her bare legs and she snapped at him. "Get down!" I wondered where she'd been all day. With Harlow Godfrey? Probably. But I wasn't supposed to care anymore.

"I already gave him a walk," I said, handing her the leash. I reached into my pocket and dug out the letter. I held it out to her, open, so she could read it.

"I found this taped to the garbage can in the park."

Lana didn't reach for the letter. She looked at it exactly like she does at Nachos when I ask her to hold her and she's got a piece of lettuce dangling off her chin. After a moment she said, "You're carrying a note from the trash around with you? Maybe you are taking this handwriting analysis thing too seriously, Anna."

"It's about Charlie. Someone thinks they recognized him. They think he's their missing dog."

Lana shook her head. "So?"

"Look, I wrote down the number of the person with the lost dog. You should call it. Or get in touch with the lady with the purple hair from the shelter and tell her about it, or something. She could call for you."

But Lana wouldn't take the letter from me. "She's on a road trip. And he's not my dog. Not really."

That made me mad. Charlie was *her* responsibility. Someone was paying her to watch him and my mom and I were getting stuck with all the work. "You might have new stuff and fancy hair, Lana, but you haven't actually changed at all. You are as self-centered as you've always been."

Lana looked at me, a flash of anger in her eyes, and her phone dinged. She glanced at it, and then squatted down to gently nudge Charlie inside. "Forget about that letter, Anna. It's probably a misunderstanding."

Back at home, Mom was packing the dog cookies into freezer bags. Each one was shaped like a little bone. Buying a bone-shaped cookie cutter had been a real waste of money. Charlie wasn't picky about what he ate. He would eat a cookie even if it was shaped like another dog. Still, I had a little sinking feeling in my chest as I pulled out the letter to show Mom. I hadn't been able to find out anything about who'd written it through handwriting analysis. And since Lana wasn't going to deal with it, I didn't really have much of a choice. It's not like I was about to meet up with some stranger in the park by myself. But I knew if Charlie went back to his real owner, all my mom's talk about me being mature and responsible enough to bike to middle school on my own would be over.

"What's this?" Mom furrowed her brow as I held up the letter. She read it as she absently plopped cookies into a freezer bag. "Oh no." She didn't say much else. Plop, plop, plop went bone-shaped cookies into the bag.

"Lana doesn't want anything to do with it," I explained.

"Hmm. There's no number or email there. How do they expect you to get in touch?"

"There was a missing dog sign next to it with a photo that looked like Charlie. I wrote down the number on the back." I flipped the letter around so she could see the number.

Mom stared at the bag of dog cookies, deep in thought. For a moment I thought she was going to ignore the letter. And I couldn't blame her. She really wanted to adopt Charlie. Then she looked up at me. "Anna, pass me my phone."

"Are you going to call Lana's mom?"

"She's so busy with work. Let's see if there's anything to this letter first. It's likely a case of mistaken identity. Small white dogs all kind of look the same from a distance."

I got the phone from the kitchen island and passed it to her. I held my breath as she dialed, thinking about how tight she squeezes Charlie and all her dorky nicknames for him. He wasn't my favourite animal, but I felt bad for her just the same. Someone must have answered because my mom talked for a few minutes about the missing dog and the note. Mom was making a plan to meet at an off-leash park. We'd drive him over. I remembered coming back from the pool and that awful smell of puke and carpet shampoo. Charlie got carsick really easily. That's why he hadn't gone on vacation with the purple-haired foster lady. Suddenly I realized that detail was important. How many cute white dogs vomit inside cars? I bet not many.

I nudged my mom. "Ask if the lost dog… what's its name? Yamiska? Ask if Yamiska gets carsick," I whispered.

My mom shushed me. I waited. Right before she was about to hang up, she mentioned how Charlie gets sick in the car and then was quiet as she listened to the response.

"Right, you mentioned that," Mom said into the phone. "Okay, well we will find out for sure on Thursday. Thanks." She hung up.

"So, who is it? What did they say about the barfing?"

"She sounds like a very old lady, Anna. She lives close to an off-leash park. Her dog got out while she was on vacation. Her niece was watching the house. She doesn't own a car, so she wasn't sure about how he does on car rides. She seemed really confused about the note. But the niece put up the missing dog signs, so maybe she wrote the note too. I'm not sure. We'll settle this all Thursday afternoon. I'll chat with Lana's mom about it too."

"Why Thursday? I wish we could get it over with today," I said.

Mom squeezed the top of the baggy closed and tossed the cookies into the freezer. "Me too. But I didn't want to push the poor woman. She sounds a little muddled. And I don't mind just a little more time with Charlie before he goes home."

That made my heart sink. A part of Mom was convinced that Charlie was Yamiska.

CHAPTER SEVENTEEN

Gifts and Inclinations

By Thursday morning I was ready to take the trailer for a test run. Mom had taken me to the store to buy a new tire. It was a little more than the money I'd saved from my job cleaning up the park for Mrs. DeJong, but Mom offered to pay the difference. I'd hoped Dad could install it, but it turns out he knows no more about basic bicycle repair than he does about flying helicopters, so I watched a few videos online and then put it on by myself, with Mom hovering over me warning me every two seconds to be careful or I'd lose a finger.

That morning, I double-checked that the trailer was attached properly to my bike so I wouldn't accidentally leave a trailer full of tortoises in my driveway. The long pole on the trailer kind of screwed into the rear axle. Since I'd already figured out how to put a wheel on, this part wasn't too tricky. The trailer seemed pretty firmly attached to my bike, but I didn't have a kickstand so the whole thing would tumble over if I didn't lean the bike against something. I'd have to remember that quirk and not leave a tortoise inside unattended. Still, I didn't want to take any chances with Nachos and Salsa, so I took the empty trailer for a test run through my neighbourhood that morning.

I could feel a breeze on my face as I whooshed down the street, with a canopy of green leaves over my head and the damp smell of sprinkler-soaked grass in the air. The trailer felt surprisingly heavy behind me, even though it was empty. I had to pedal extra hard and when I reached a corner, I needed to take wide turns.

Biking that day, I kind of felt like a balloon filling up with helium. Happy and full. Nachos and Salsa would soon be on the road to the vet with me. I'd keep my tortoises and my freedoms, like biking to middle school and maybe even to Putter's Paradise. I pushed away the troubling thought that Lana's amazing minigolf talents were going to waste in her current best friend situation. The other problem bothering me a little was Charlie. If the dog ended up being Yamiska, I wouldn't be going anywhere without Mom tailing me. But I had a bike trailer! I'd found it and fixed it up myself. I pedaled home fast, excited to take Salsa for a test ride.

When I pulled up to my house, Mom and Dad were coming out the door. Mom had Charlie in her arms. I was grinning like crazy and was surprised that Dad was home. I wanted to show off the trailer, but then I saw how grim they both looked and remembered that it was time to meet the old lady with the missing dog in the off-leash park.

"Snazzy trailer," said Dad. I slowly got off my bike to keep it from falling over, but of course it tumbled over with a clatter. Luckily, it was empty.

"I remember when you used to ride around in one of those," said Mom, glancing at the trailer. Everything seems to remind Mom of when I was little. If I parachuted out of an airplane, she'd tell me about how I used to jump off the bed holding a pillowcase. Mom looked down at Charlie and gave him a snuggle. He licked her face and she turned to Dad. "We should bring some towels in case he vomits."

Dad unlocked his car with the remote. "He pukes during car rides? No one mentioned that pertinent detail before."

"I'll get the old towels," I said. But while I was trying to remember where Mom kept them, I suddenly recalled the fib I told her about why I was fixing up the bike trailer. "Why don't I take him in the bike trailer instead? He might not get sick with all the fresh air and it's much slower than a car."

"That's worth a try, Anna," said Dad. "Do a spin around here first and see if he likes it."

I set the bike and trailer up again. Mom unzipped the trailer flap and gently placed Charlie inside, then zipped it up again. I could see his little face looking out the mesh window. He licked it. Disgusting. Our street was quiet, so I biked down it for half a block, then made a wide turn in the road and biked back again. After I pulled over, I held up the bike so it wouldn't tumble over while I did a quick over-the-shoulder vomit check on Charlie. He was wagging his tail, his wet nose poked up against the mesh window. No puke.

"He seems to like the trailer," Mom said. She checked the time on her phone. "We're almost late and this lady doesn't have a cellphone. We'll get going now and let her know that you will be coming a little later with Charlie."

I couldn't believe what I was hearing. Mom was going to let me bike all the way to the off-leash park by myself. It would be the longest distance I had ever gone on my own. I glanced at Dad, who winked at me, and then they headed to the car. I waited for them to pull out. I hopped on my bike and started to pedal, the trailer dragging a little more because of the weight of the dog.

"Hold on tight, Charlie," I shouted.

During the bike ride to the park, I forget for a moment about Charlie and how we might lose him. I just enjoyed the sound of my tires on the pavement and the distant smell of a backyard barbecue. I braked at the busy street and walked my bike across once the cars stopped, feeling I should take extra care because I was responsible for Charlie. I could see with a glance over my shoulder that he had his tongue out, which gave him an expression that almost looked like a big grin. I was sure he could smell the smoke of barbecues too.

It was a long ride, about fifteen minutes, and when I turned into the gravel lot for the dog park, I could see lots of parked vehicles. The off-leash area was busy with larger dogs running around, leaping at each other, and chasing balls. I stopped the bike and leaned it against the fence. I could see my parents now, standing with an older woman in a green coat. Dad waved.

I unzipped the big flap on the trailer and pulled Charlie out, carrying him in my arms through the gate and into the dog park. With all the big dogs running around, I felt a little worried for him. The top of his curly white head smelled sweet, like baby shampoo. I felt strange, almost sad. I realized that I didn't want Mom to lose Charlie. Not at all. And it had nothing to do with me no longer getting treated like a little kid. I wished, for a moment, that I had never found that note. Then I looked up and saw the lady.

She was smiling hopefully at Charlie, and she had short-ish grey curls and wrinkles around her eyes. I hugged him a little tighter.

"This is Mrs. Lee," my mom said. "This is Anna, and our Charlie, umm, I mean the stray dog we are helping look after."

I put Charlie down and he ran straight to Mrs. Lee. He sniffed her shoes and wagged his little tail, then tried to jump up on her pants. She stepped back and frowned. He tried to jump up on her again. "No," she said firmly, and she stepped back again. "Bad dog." Charlie sat down and cocked his head. Then he jumped on her again. "This isn't my Yamiska," Mrs. Lee snapped. "Yamiska had much better manners. You need to train this dog."

Mom's mouth dropped open a little. I could see she was torn between relief and shock at the lady's rude tone. But Dad spoke before Mom said something she'd regret. "I'm so sorry we got your hopes up, Mrs. Lee. You must miss Yamiska very much."

"I do. Very much. He kept me active. I walked with him every day and that gave me people to talk to."

"Why don't you get a new dog?" I asked. Mom shot me a you're-being-rude look. She usually saves that for parent-teacher interviews.

"I'm too old to train another dog," Mrs. Lee said. "It's a lot of work. You see with this animal what happens when you don't put in the time."

Mom reached down and gave Charlie a scratch. "Well, I could do with a little advice on training, Mrs. Lee. Would you like to meet me for walks? We can meet right here since it's close to your house."

"I'd like that." She reached down and gave Charlie a pet. "He seems biddable."

My parents and Mrs. Lee started chatting about word commands and dog treats so I stopped listening. I was thinking about the handwriting I had analyzed. The person who wrote that note didn't seem at all like Mrs. Lee. This old lady wasn't all over the place. She seemed like someone who had firmly made up her mind about dog training and probably a whole lot of other things too. I interrupted Mom. "Mrs. Lee? Someone left me a note on a trash can. Was it your niece?"

The old lady looked confused. "That careless young woman? No. She put up some signs when Yamiska went missing. But she flew home weeks ago."

"And you didn't write the note?"

"What note?"

I felt a little dizzy for a moment. Our dog wasn't Yamiska and someone else had gone to all of the trouble of leaving a note on a trash bin pretending to be Yamiska's owner. I really wanted to bike home and look at the note, to search it again for clues. But I couldn't interrupt Mom, who seemed to be happily chatting with Mrs. Lee. My mom is really an old lady inside. She can't wait to spend her days gardening and telling kids not to be so loud and dogs not to be so rude.

CHAPTER EIGHTEEN

Signs of Forgery

Dad grilled up pancakes on Friday morning in his bathrobe. Mom sipped coffee on the kitchen island, nervously chattering on about her job interview. I stared down at my tortoise-shaped pancake, feeling guilty, knowing I had to bring up the tricky topic of the vet appointment.

"Don't forget Nachos and Salsa have a checkup today," I finally said. "At 11 a.m."

"But that's when I have my interview," Mom said. She turned to Dad. "Can you take her?"

Dad pointed his pancake flipper at me. "Can't. I'm in meetings. You should have brought this up sooner, Anna. We'll need to reschedule it."

"But Dr. O'Sullivan is booked for weeks," I fibbed. "I can take them in the bike trailer. It's closer than the dog park I took Charlie to yesterday."

Mom and Dad exchanged a look. "Are you sure it's not too far?" Dad said.

"I can handle this. Don't worry."

Mom looked doubtful. "We've put this off for so long and Frank's been asking if the tortoises are healthy."

My guilt vanished at the mention of Dad's old room-mate's name.

"The best I can do is move some things around at work and make sure I'm there to meet her to settle the bill at the end," Dad said, adding a pancake to Mom's plate. "It's just a checkup. Anna can handle the vet part. And that way I can skip the chit chat."

"The snake chit chat?" I said.

Dad shivered. "Yes, that's the part I won't mind missing."

Alone in the house with Nachos and Salsa that morning, I stared at the mysterious note. I tried squinting, holding it upside down, looking at it from far away. I realize these are not real graphology techniques, but this was not a real handwriting sample. It was a fake. I bet real graphologists were in great demand back in the olden days when people wrote everything by hand, like ransom notes and millionaire wills. Police probably needed professional help spotting the imposters. That made me realize there had to be something in the book about fakes. I'd read less than half of the book. There were chapters and chapters more to go, filled with lots of advice and handwriting samples. I flipped through, trying to find something about fakes. I got all the way to the end and nothing. But then I noticed the index. There was a list of topics under "F." I didn't find "Fakes," but I found "Forgeries" and a page number.

Basically, the author of the book wrote that if some-one is going to fake their handwriting, they are going to have to write slowly, and even then it's hard to disguise the small things that make a person's handwriting unique: how they connect letters, how wide each letter is, how much space the upper and lower parts of their letters take up between the ruled lines. Those are all super unique. I figured there had to be a clue like that in the note from "a sad dog owner."

But no matter how hard I examined the writing, I couldn't figure this note out. Nothing really stood out as unique. I'd find something, like an extra loopy letter, but then look for a match somewhere else in the note and discover that whoever wrote it did something different in the next line. Finally, I gave up and went over to check on Nachos, who was hiding in her box. The basking lamp cast a warm glow over the dirt, the plants, and the mucky water. I'd meant to clean that water every day. I lifted the box up and there was Nachos, all tucked up, her shell looking worse where the crack was. Something smelly was just barely oozing out of it.

"Oh no, poor Nachos," I said. "You haven't given this to Salsa, have you?"

I anxiously turned to Salsa in the kiddy pool. She nibbled on a small chunk of carrot. Salsa seemed okay. Then I turned back to Nachos. I'd been taking good care of her, hadn't I? I'd talked to her, fed her, and carried her to the park. I'd fixed up a bike trailer for her. I'd booked the vet appointment. Then I saw that dirty water and I decided I'd better give both tortoises some fresher water right away. And I hadn't cleaned the habitats. I'd gotten a little distracted fixing up the bike trailer and sorting out the truth behind Charlie and the mystery note. I had two hours until the vet appointment. I had time to clean both habitats.

I carried Salsa out to the garage to look for containers big enough to put them in while I cleaned. As soon as

I flipped on the light, I admired my bike trailer. Then I put Salsa down on the cement floor and dug through the recycling bin until I found a box that had once held a pair of Mom's winter boots. Each separate side was big enough for a Hermann's tortoise. They would probably fit well in the bike trailer too. When I turned around, Salsa wasn't where I'd left her. She'd waddled closer to the garage door. I scooped Salsa up and slipped her inside one of the boxes, unzipped the bike trailer and then tucked the box into the bottom, snug under the bench seat so it wouldn't bounce around. I wasn't sure how I'd fit two boxes in such a small space, but I'd figure that out later.

On the way back to my room, I checked the clock in the kitchen.

"Plenty of time to clean," I told Salsa, who looked relaxed in her box.

As I emptied out the habitats and scrubbed each one down with tortoise-safe cleaner, I thought about the note. Who had written it? I wasn't much of a graphologist if I couldn't solve a simple case of forgery. I must be missing something.

The note was still face down on the carpet, next to the paddling pool. Once I had finished cleaning and had returned Salsa and Nachos to their separate habitats, I picked it up, scanning each word for clues. I reached into the habitat to scratch Nachos on her shell, avoiding the bad spot.

I still couldn't find any clue that would help solve the mystery.

Nachos began to wander away from under my hand. I glanced over at her and thought about how her shell always reminded me of a bowl of tortilla chips, then looked back at the page. Suddenly I realized something I hadn't seen before about the small letter 'A' at the end of the name Yamiska. It had a tiny hook that pointed back to the word, a strange quirk I'd seen somewhere else.

Maybe in the book.

I flipped through *The Guide to Graphology*, landing on the section with drawings of different ways people write each letter and hunted through the page on 'A.' There it was—the hook meant a sense of self-importance. Where had I seen that? I pulled out my stack of handwriting samples and flipped through each one, hunting for the letter: Maddison, nope; Evan, nope; Dad, nope. Finally, Lana, and there it was.

That quirky letter A belonged to Lana.

It was right there in her name on the contract she'd copied out in the first week of summer break.

Lana had written the note!

Selfish Lana and that stupid note had almost ruined everything. She'd nearly had Charlie stolen from us, along with my one chance to have a little bit of freedom. And Lana had made me look foolish in front of Evan, Maddison, my parents—everybody. I scrunched up the piece of paper and tossed it across the room. It hit the wall and bounced back down, landing softly on the carpet.

I felt like tearing the note into a thousand pieces, but even more, I felt like confronting Lana about her trickery. And I wanted to do it now.

I glanced back at my sick tortoise. I felt torn between my anger at Lana and needing to help Nachos. I looked at the clock. If I took Nachos to Lana's house, I could still get her to the vet by 11 a.m. But I didn't have enough time to figure out how to load them both into the trailer safely and I couldn't put them in the same box. Salsa, who was healthy, could go another day.

I grabbed Lana's fake note and slid it under my armpit, put Nachos in a box and marched out to the garage.

CHAPTER NINETEEN

Mastery of Analysis

A t Lana's house I steadied my bike against the lamp pole and told Nachos I'd be right back. I ran up to the front door, ringing the doorbell three times quick. Lana's mom answered.

"I need to speak to Lana," I said.

"She's out with a friend," her mom replied, her tone a little too sympathetic for my liking. "I dropped Lana off at the minigolf place less than an hour ago."

"Putter's Paradise?" I couldn't believe it. Lana was at *our* place with Harlow Godfrey. I felt even angrier.

"You could call her on her phone," Lana's mom shouted as I ran back to my bike. "Do you have the number?"

"No. This is something that needs to be said in person," I shouted back.

I pedaled hard, not really thinking about how far it was to Putter's Paradise. After accidentally hitting a rock in the road or taking a too-tight turn, I shouted apologies back at poor Nachos, whose boot box bumped around in the back. Lana and Harlow were minigolfing together. I thought Lana didn't even like minigolf anymore. All the little things Lana had done that summer had added up, like the strokes of the letters connecting a word, and I could see the meaning hidden in the handwriting. And I didn't like what it meant.

I rounded a corner and saw the Putter's Paradise sign and the tips of the blades on the windmill. I turned into the driveway and biked past the clubhouse where you rent the balls and the clubs. A few families and a pair of teenagers were playing. I couldn't spot Lana and Harlow but that wasn't surprising because the golf course kind of crisscrossed around the miniature buildings and the mucky stream with the wooden bridges. You couldn't see everybody on all eighteen holes at the same time. I looked forward to telling Lana and Harlow exactly what I thought of them. I hopped off my bike and wheeled it onto the grass, where I gently let it down. The trailer stayed upright. There, under a tree, I spotted Lana's mom's picnic blanket with the purple and green stripes. Charlie was tied up to the tree near a sign that read: "No dogs." When he saw me, he tugged on the short leash and wagged his tail like crazy. I was worried the bike trailer would eventually tip over, so I unzipped the bike trailer's door flap and fished out the box with Nachos inside. I gently placed the box on Lana's blanket, far away from Charlie, who was now whimpering with excitement.

"Stay," I said to both the tortoise and dog as I dug the letter out of my pocket. "I'll be right back."

I marched through the minigolf course along the winding gravel path, angry words about Lana and Harlow filling my head and crowding out all the things that I usually love about the place. By the eleventh hole I spotted Lana. She was smiling, swinging her club back and forth. Her shorter hair was pulled back into a mini ponytail and she was wearing a new summer dress with tiny flowers all over it. I knew that a miniature castle, under which the ball was supposed to roll, sat at the other end of the green. I expected Harlow Godfrey there, towering over the crumbling fairytale castle like a toothy giant. But as the path twisted around the corner, I realized it wasn't Harlow. I recognized, with a sharp intake of breath, that it was Evan. He was focusing on his ball, which was near the little hole. He held a putter in both hands and his dark hair hung into his eyes. He swung and the ball landed in the hole. I felt confused.

Were Evan and Lana alone? At Putter's Paradise?

Was it a date? That word felt like a punch in the gut.

I didn't know what to say so I held up the letter and shouted. "Lana, you tricked me!"

Lana looked up at me, confused. Then she noticed the paper in my hand and her expression switched to guilt. "What took you so long to figure it out?"

Evan noticed me and said, "Hey Anna. What's going on?"

I ignored the traitor. I kept shouting at Lana instead. "So you admit it? My mom got really upset. She called some old stranger lady and got her all excited that Charlie was her dog. And now they are friends. Friends! You are a selfish, self-centered person."

Lana leaned on her club. "Your mom has a new pal. And she'll still adopt Charlie. Both of those things mean she won't be staring over your shoulder all the time. That doesn't sound so bad. Besides, I told you to forget about the letter. You weren't supposed to take it that far. You were supposed to figure it out right away. You're always bragging about how well you know me and what a super talented handwriting analyzer person you are."

"A graphologist!" I shouted.

"Don't yell at me," said Lana. Her eyes got watery. "You never stop and take the time to hear me. I can't even finish a sentence."

"Forget it," I said. "We're not friends anymore and it's all your fault." But even as the words came out of my mouth, I regretted them. I didn't want to lose Lana as a friend. I wanted everything to go back to the way it was. Back when my mom had her old job and we were still in elementary school and Nachos wasn't sick. I wanted it all back. Then the thought of Nachos and her oozing shell made me suddenly remember, with a sinking kind of dread, that I was supposed to take her to the vet.

"Wait. What time is it?" I said.

Lana pulled her phone out of the pocket on her dress. "It's 10:35."

"I still have time." I thought about her phone, how I could use it to call and explain where I was and get Dad to help me. But I didn't want to use Lana's stupid new phone, didn't want to tell Dad the truth, and I had just enough time to make it to the vet alone.

I ran back toward the grassy picnic area. When I got to the blanket, Charlie ran toward me, going nuts wagging his tail. Why wasn't he tied up? The leash was still tied to the tree, still attached to the collar. He'd yanked on it until his collar had slipped off. And the box was on its side. Nachos wasn't inside. She wasn't on the blanket. Confused, I scanned the grass, expecting to find her camouflaged among the green blades. But no Nachos.

Lana and Evan came up behind me, each holding a putter and a golf ball.

"Nachos is gone," I said. "I don't know how she got out of the box."

"Your tortoise was here?" said Evan, looking around. "Wait, isn't Nachos the sick one?"

"I'm supposed to take Nachos to the vet. If my parents find out what's happening they'll be so mad. They'll give Nachos and Salsa back to Dad's old roommate."

Lana widened her eyes. "Your parents can't give Nachos and Salsa away. You've had them forever."

I glared at her. "You don't even like them, Lana."

Evan tossed his putter and ball into the grass. "I bet Charlie accidentally tipped over the box when he pulled himself loose. Let's split up and find Nachos. I mean, how far could she have gotten?"

"Tortoises move faster than you'd expect," I said.

"What if someone stole her?" Lana said, tossing aside her putter and ball too and untying Charlie's leash from the tree, presumably so she could slip the collar back on the dog, who was unhelpfully licking my ankles.

"Don't say stuff like that," said Evan. "Just look for her."

I hunted through the grass, trying to imagine where Nachos would go. Which direction? There was a row of low shrubs and I thought maybe she might have hidden under them, so I got down on my knees and stared, pushing aside the branches with my hands, calling "Nachos, here Nachos." It smelled damp and it was cool under the bush. Perfect spot for a hiding tortoise. My throat tightened up. I forced myself not to cry. I had really messed everything up. I had lost Lana. I had lost Nachos and now, even if I found her, it might be too late and I'd be caught in my lies. Mom and Dad would make me get rid of Nachos and Salsa. Everything had changed and no matter how hard I tried, I couldn't stop it.

Nachos wasn't under the shrubs.

I worried for a moment that she had made it all the way to the muddy stream. Maybe she had been thirsty. But the water was moving too fast and was too deep for a tortoise. She could drown. I stood up and started to run towards the stream, imagining only the worst. Then I heard Lana's voice, calling me.

Lana stood in the grass, closer to where I'd left my bike. She had Charlie on the leash.

"I found her!" she shouted. "She's okay, but look." She pointed and grinned.

I got near and I realized why Lana was smiling. Nachos was crouched in the grass, relaxed, sunning herself. She was pressed up against what looked like a green dome. It was a lawn sprinkler, built into the ground.

"That thing looks exactly like a turtle. I think she misses Salsa," said Lana. "I didn't know Nachos could travel that far so quickly."

"I've told you a million times that tortoises are faster than you'd expect. And how could you leave Charlie tied up with a loose collar like that? He slipped away so easily."

Lana looked hurt. "Now it's my fault Nachos went missing? You blame me for everything."

I scooped up Nachos and gently hugged her. "You're right. I should never have brought her here. And I should never have left her alone."

We walked through the grass together toward the bike

trailer. Somewhere out here, Evan was still looking for Nachos. Lana pulled out her phone and showed me it was 10:52. "You'll never make it to the vet in time."

I realized, with a rising sense of dread, that I had to call Dad at work. I knew I'd be in big trouble for hiding Nachos' injury, lying about the vet being booked solid, and riding out alone to Putter's Paradise, but Nachos' health was more important than all that. "Pass me your phone. I need to call my parents."

"Sure," she said, handing it over.

But I had to know one thing before I dialed. "Why is Evan here with you?"

Lana blushed. "Because I helped him fix his bike. He said you kept putting him off. Don't worry. It's not a date."

I had totally forgotten about my promise to fix his bike.

CHAPTER TWENTY

Graphological Exercises

D ad was standing, arms crossed, in the driveway when I pulled up, my thighs aching and my forehead all sweaty under the helmet.

"I'm furious about this," he said. "I already have Salsa in the car. Is Nachos in the trailer? Is she okay?"

I couldn't even look at Dad. "Sorry, I made a big mistake. And I tried to get here as fast as I could but we're really late."

"Well let's hope Dr. O'Sullivan can squeeze us in," he said. And we were both quiet after he said that because we were thinking about the vet's anaconda.

Dr. O'Sullivan is not a dog person. She is not a cat person. She's not even a tortoise person. She's a snake person. She has glass cages full of horrible, slithery snakes stacked up all over her cramped waiting room. My dad can't even look at them without shuddering. Dr. O'Sullivan is always complaining about how when the news covers a snake escape, they get the breed wrong. Every time she says this, I look around and I worry about the chances of *her* snakes escaping. She doesn't seem as invested in tortoise misidentifications, but Dad said he's looked around and she's well qualified to be a vet to Nachos and Salsa, and the office is nearby, so that's why we always end up at Dr. O'Sullivan's.

I carried Nachos from the waiting room into the examination room, strategically avoiding a tattooed guy coming out with a small yellow snake wrapped around his wrist. Dad carried Salsa. The room had an island in the middle of it for pets, so I carefully placed Nachos down on it.

"Shell rot, all the classic signs," said Dr. O'Sullivan once she started the examination. She scraped at the bad patch with a little tool she'd dug out of her lab coat pocket. "You've been keeping the area clean?"

Dad sideways glanced at me. "The cage or the shell?"

"Both." Dr. O'Sullivan went over to the counter and pulled out a bottle. She opened it and dabbed the contents on a cotton pad. Then she rubbed it on Nachos' shell. "You've separated this tortoise from the other one?"

"Yes, I did," I said, glancing at Salsa in Dad's hands. "And I cleaned both habitats this morning."

"I'll examine the other one next, just to be sure. The longer you leave something like this festering, the more likely you're going to see a systemic infection. It can be fatal. You'll need an ointment and instructions."

I felt a wave of shock. "Fatal? Like she could die?"

"If not taken care of properly, of course," the vet said. Dr. O'Sullivan walked over to a cabinet and opened it, fished around, and pulled out a tube of goop. "Who should I give this to?"

"Me," I said. "I'm going get Nachos better."

"This is serious now, Anna," Dad said, but he took the tube from the vet and handed it to me.

I held it tightly, knowing that I couldn't keep ignoring my responsibilities towards the tortoises.

Adults are always complaining that a doctor's handwriting on prescriptions is hard to read, but have you ever seen a vet's? At the end of our visit, Dr. O'Sullivan handed us a prescription with directions for putting the medicine on Nachos, and I took one look at her scratchy, scrunched up letters and decided that only a professional graphologist —or at least someone who had finished the entire book— could decipher it. But I'd been paying attention to her spoken instructions and I knew I could help Nachos.

After we were in the car, Dad turned to me. "You deceived us and it could have ended badly for Nachos."

"I shouldn't have lied," I said. "It was selfish of me. I promise to take care of her. You heard the vet, she could die. I wouldn't let that happen." And I meant it.

"I believe you Anna, but you need to convince your mom too."

We were both quiet as Dad started the drive home, but after a while he spoke. "I've got a new tortoise idiom for you. *Travel at your own pace, you'll always arrive.*"

I didn't say anything. I was too busy deciding on my destination.

Once we got home, I sat on the floor beside the living room couch and thought about all the mistakes I'd made and how I *had* to become a better tortoise caretaker. Frank's petting farm would be a horrible fate. Nachos and Salsa needed me to be better.

I'd gotten *The Guide to Graphology* from my bedroom, along with a pad of paper and a pencil. I ran my fingers along the gold lettering on the book's spine. Then I wrote the sentence that Dad had spoken in the car: *Travel at your own pace, you'll always arrive.*

I had never analyzed my own handwriting. I already knew that I had large handwriting and I'd read somewhere in the book that oversized writing is a good thing. I turned to that page.

"Amplified writing portrays confidence, ambition, and enthusiasm," the author wrote. That was definitely me. But I guess I didn't read the whole section before, because it went on to say: "The writer also suffers from a lack consideration of others, displaying carelessness and a tendency towards bossiness." And even worse, it meant I could easily be distracted, so distracted that I didn't even manage to cross my capital "T" properly. The stroke kind of dashed off ahead of the rest of the letter, meaning I'm quick thinking but my thoughts kind of get ahead of me, "demonstrating an inclination to hastiness and subsequent neglect of the extras."

Mom found me chewing on the end of the pencil, thinking about how that handwriting analysis book was frustrating. It would tell you one thing and then flip around and tell you the opposite. It didn't make any sense. On the way back from the job interview, Mom had stopped off at Lana's to pick up Charlie, who now nuzzled my knee then curled up next to me.

"I heard about Nachos," she said. "We're disappointed that you hid her injury from us and that you weren't honest about the time of the appointment you had booked."

I looked up at Mom, but I was still thinking about my handwriting. "I showed a lack of consideration for others, and I was kind of neglectful and careless. I'm sorry."

I tried to give Charlie a scratch behind his ear, but he flipped over on his back so I gave him a belly rub instead.

Mom was quiet for a while, watching Charlie. "Dad told me all about Frank's petting farm. It seems like a poor fit. That got me thinking that I could be on board with keeping those tortoises."

"I won't make the same mistakes," I said. "I'll look after Nachos and Salsa properly."

Mom reached over and wrapped her arm around my shoulder, giving me a squeeze.

"There's some good news today—I got that job. The thing is, I won't be home as much as I thought to look after Charlie. And it made me realize that I hadn't been very fair. If we are going to adopt a dog, I think we should *all* want to adopt a dog."

I rubbed Charlie's tummy a little more. I was surprised that Mom was asking me. I hadn't wanted Charlie around at first and she knew it. But so much had changed.

"Let's do it. He's good buddies with Nachos and Salsa now."

Mom smiled and looked at my piece of paper. "What are you writing there?"

"Can people be two things at once?" I asked her. "Can somebody be something good, like confident, and something not so great, like bossy, at the same time?"

I was thinking about graphology, but Mom didn't know that. "Hmm, I haven't thought about that. But I don't think people fit into easy little categories. People are complex. We just need to try our best every day. We're all still learning."

Were we all a little bit mixed up inside? Was it okay to be a little bit of both? When I was analyzing Lana's handwriting, why did I focus on the negative things and not see the good things too? Handwriting analysis was getting me all jumbled up and not thinking about the important stuff, like tortoises and friendships, at all. I'd heard kids in Finland didn't even learn cursive. They had typing classes instead. So maybe writing in cursive really was an obsolete skill, like learning to square dance or knowing how to fold a map.

CHAPTER TWENTY-ONE

Practical Applications of Graphology

A few days later, Lana called me to ask me if we could meet at Putter's Paradise, which surprised me. I didn't think it would be fun to bike alone so I called Evan. He agreed to bike with me if I didn't tease him for riding on the sidewalk. I told him I'd ride on the sidewalk too, as long as there was enough room for the bike trailer, which I was going to load up with treats. And I had to give Maddison my analysis of her handwriting, so I also invited her.

Before I left, I checked on Nachos. Her shell was looking better. I had applied the goop every day, as well as kept her shell and the habitat extra clean. The smelly gunk was gone and her shell was starting to look normal again.

Then I got a picnic blanket and all the things we would need for a picnic lunch from our pantry: chips, fruit rolls, fizzy water in cans, fancy crackers, and a chocolate bar. Charlie was jumping all over me, sniffing curiously at the stuff I was putting into a bag.

"Why don't you bring him?" Mom said.

"Maddison is allergic to dogs and they aren't allowed on the greens," I explained as much to Charlie as to Mom. "I promise to give you a big w-a-l-k when I get home." I spelled it out so he wouldn't get excited. We were always doing that. He hadn't gotten any brighter since I first met him. You would think he could spell a simple word like walk by now.

When we arrived at Putter's Paradise, Evan and I carried my picnic stuff to the shady spot under the elm tree that had the best view of the fake greens. That's where we were all going to meet. I spread out the blanket. I thought about the fall and how I was still pretty nervous about coming out of my own comfy shell.

"When we get to middle school, are you going to eat lunch with me?" I asked Evan.

"What about Lana?" he said. "You always eat lunch with her."

"Lana's probably going to do her own thing," I said. "You can do what you want too, I guess. Just promise you will eat with me on the first day, so I don't have to eat alone. Only the first day. I mean who else would you eat lunch with?"

"We can eat lunch together," he said. "But stop acting like you're my only friend. I have friends from school. We game online together. That's not your thing, I know, but I like it."

"Really?" I was going to say that I thought he was in his basement all the time because he is lonely and weird, but I remembered how I was only seeing one side of things when I was studying handwriting. It might seem lonely and weird to me to have friends that you rarely hang out with in person, but Evan was kind of shy, and if it worked for him, then why should I make him feel bad about it? "Thanks for agreeing to eat lunch with me," I told him.

Lana showed up next. She was texting someone while she walked through the grass and nearly bumped into a tree. Evan snorted with laughter.

"I'm going to the clubhouse to see if I can get a better putter than I got last time," Evan said. "Lana kicked my butt."

"You won't beat her no matter what kind of putter you get. She's too good," I said.

Lana smiled at me and awkwardly said hello to Evan, blushing a little as he walked past her.

Once Evan was far enough away that he couldn't hear us Lana said, "I've been meaning to say, I'm sorry I wrote that note. Especially because of your mom. She really loves Charlie. I didn't think it through. You weren't hearing me when I tried to explain that I've changed. I thought you'd read the letter and you'd learn that I can be different. That I can change as easily as my handwriting. But you came to my house and you said those mean things about me. I got so mad that I didn't tell you the truth. And then everything got out of hand."

"Charlie's not so bad," I said. Now that she'd apologized, I felt like I had to say sorry too, but it was hard. "I don't think my analysis of your handwriting was very accurate because it was my first one. I was still trying to improve my technique." I took a deep breath. Sometimes you know you're supposed to stop talking, and you keep telling yourself you should stop talking, but it's like some-one is unravelling all your thoughts and you can't keep them in. "Evan says I'm not intuitive, that I don't really understand people. But I don't know. When I studied your handwriting, it made me think about how you are starting to be more interested in things I'm not inter-ested in…." I had written in my analysis that Lana was self-centered, but now I realized what I meant was she wasn't Anna-centered. "It's not that you only think about yourself. Not exactly. It's that you barely ever think about me anymore."

Lana frowned. "We're not the same person, Anna. 'Banana Twins' was funny when we were little, but we're going to middle school soon. We've outgrown it."

"I know that. But why can't things stay the same?" I said. "You're going to hang out with that toothy giraffe Harlow Godfrey and forget all about me."

"That's not a nice thing to say about Harlow," said Lana. "And you can't freeze time. We're always going to be friends, but I'm allowed to make new friends too and eat lunch with other people and join, I don't know, the algebra club, if I want to."

I chuckled a little. Lana was so terrible at algebra. But I stopped myself from saying anything because I didn't want to argue with her anymore. Just imagining Lana eating lunch with someone else at middle school gave me a sinking feeling. But I knew I couldn't hold on to her so tightly anymore. It wasn't making either of us happy.

"We'll still be friends, no matter who we eat lunch with?" I asked.

"But you must promise not to be rude to Harlow," she said.

Luckily, somebody sneezed.

"Fresh cut grass," explained Maddison as she walked over to us. Evan, behind her, twirled his putter around in circles. Maddison pulled a tissue out of her pocket. Then she launched into a long speech about pollens. Lana pretended to be interested, but she was playing with her hair and kept glancing over at Evan, who completely ignored her. This whole Lana-around-Evan thing was annoying, but the new me was going to let them deal with it and not get involved.

"Have you analyzed my handwriting sample yet, Anna?" Maddison asked.

Evan groaned. "You don't believe in that pseudoscientific stuff, do you?"

I crouched down to pull my handwriting analysis book out of my bag. Maddison's sample was tucked inside, along with her five dollars that I intended to return to her, and a pencil to mark the page. Lana grabbed the book from me and smiled. "Not this book again."

"Give it back," I said.

"First, I'm going to do an experiment," she said. "We'll each write a note for you and you need to figure out who wrote it."

"I didn't bring any paper."

"We can write in your book."

"Fine. But do it on the inside cover so you don't mess up the real pages."

Lana wrote something, then passed it to Evan, who read hers and slightly nodded. Then Maddison wrote something. I didn't understand why they were even doing it. Of course, I could tell their handwriting apart. I had spent enough time staring at it.

I took the book from Maddison. "This is a very valuable, rare book," I said. "And now you guys have scribbled graffiti all over it."

Lana smiled. "Just guess who is who."

The first scribble said: *Anna makes me feel brave.* I grinned at Lana. "This one is yours. I can tell from the slant in your letters that being adventurous is one of your strongest traits."

Evan had printed in capital letters: *Anna can be insightful... when she wants to be.* I smirked. "Evan, it's clear from your blocky letters that you have a scientific mind."

The last one had to be Maddison's. She'd written: *It's good to have a new friend who is funny and has cute tortoises.* I thanked her and gave her the handwriting analysis and the five-dollar bill. I had been careful to think of her feelings when I wrote it up. I'm not sure if this graphology thing really works, but handing people a list of their least attractive personality traits is a sure way to lose them.

"This is for you, Maddison. You don't need to pay me. You're my friend. Besides, you're the only one here who is good at following instructions."

Maddison smiled as she read her handwriting analysis. I held my book tight to my chest, feeling good about the fresh handwriting samples on the inside cover. I might fail to properly cross my T's and be too hasty. Narrow letters may show I'm full of avarice, whatever that means. Knotted, large loopy letters probably show pride in my own achievements. I'm a little bossy, a little hasty, and a little self-centered. Or maybe I'm really confident, really ambitious, and really enthusiastic. On the first day of middle school, I can choose who I want to be. My own handwriting is all over the place anyway.

The End